Some Lies Will Haunt You

JANE BLYTHE

Cover designed by Q Designs

Created with Vellum

Acknowledgments

I'd like to thank everyone who played a part in bringing this story to life. Particularly my mom who is always there to share her thoughts and opinions with me. My wonderful cover designer Amy who did an amazing job with this stunning cover. My fabulous editor Lisa for all the hard work she puts into polishing my work. My awesome team, Sophie, Robyn, and Clayr, without your help I'd never be able to run my street team. And my fantastic street team members who help share my books with every share, comment, and like!

And of course a big thank you to all of you, my readers! Without you I wouldn't be living my dreams of sharing the stories in my head with the world!

CHAPTER *One*

April 5th
3:42 A.M.

Maggie Wilson woke with a start, not quite sure what had yanked her out of sleep.

It was probably nothing.

She was the world's lightest sleeper, and it wasn't like she had any real motivation to stay asleep anyway. Her sleep was always plagued with nightmares.

Always.

Every single night for as many of her twenty-seven years that she could remember, she'd had bad dreams. As a child, she used to be terrified to go to bed each night, knowing what was waiting for her as soon as she laid her head down on the pillow and closed her eyes.

Somniphobia.

It was one of the hardest things in the world to have a phobia of sleep.

Damned if you did and damned if you didn't.

The human body needed sleep to function so giving it up wasn't an option, but sleeping hurt her so much more than anything else ever could.

All she had ever wanted in her whole life was one blissful night of uninterrupted sleep. No dreams. No nightmares. No thrashing as she fought against a monster that didn't exist. No waking with a scream dying on her lips. Just peaceful, quiet sleep like everyone else had.

Tonight was obviously not going to be the night she got her wish.

Reaching over, Maggie picked up her cell phone from the nightstand and looked at the time. It was quarter to four in the morning, much earlier than she usually awoke.

Since sleep wasn't something she enjoyed, she stuck to a very strict regime. She'd lie down at nine on the dot, usually she would be awake by eleven with a bad dream. She'd get up, drink a glass of cold water to calm down, and then take a hot shower because she would more often than not wake in a panic, covered in a sheen of sweat. After that, she'd read a chapter or two of whatever book she was reading at the time, then take a sleeping pill and sleep through till six.

That was two hours away.

With a growing sense of unease that maybe something really had woken her up, Maggie sat up and switched on the lamp beside her bed. She always slept with both a nightlight on—so she wasn't completely in the dark—and the TV on—so things weren't completely quiet—the room had had light but not enough to properly see if something—some*one*—was in here with her.

It was stupid, she knew that, but she was such a creature of routine that the fact she had slept only three hours when she should have gotten at least five with the help of the pills, was making her nervous.

Carefully, she scanned the room, besides her bed and the nightstands on either side of it, there was a dresser and a wardrobe, nothing else, so not a lot of places to hide, and she didn't see anything that looked out of the ordinary.

"Great," she muttered to herself. "Now your dream monsters are chasing you into the real world."

It was bad enough that her sleep was haunted by evil people from her past and the lies that she had told without her waking life being invaded by those same memories.

She needed to be able to function.

She needed to keep the past in the past.

No matter how hard it was, that was where the past belonged, she couldn't change it—no matter how much she wanted to—and she couldn't erase the scars it had left on her soul and her psyche, so she had to keep moving forward. She did the best she could, she owned a successful hotel, she had a few friends who she cherished, she enjoyed the small things in life, like a sunset, or the sound of the water in the river that ran along the back of her property, or the smell of freshly cut grass.

Yet she didn't feel like she was really living.

She was merely marking time until the inevitable end of her life.

Throwing back the covers, Maggie climbed out of bed before she could get too philosophical. What was, was, and she had to make the best of it.

Since she was up now, whether because she'd woken on her own or because of something else, she may as well get started on her day. Most days Maggie made sure she was dressed, with her hair and makeup done, and down in the kitchen by the time the staff started arriving at half-past six. The dining room opened for guests to start having breakfast at seven, and although she had staff to take care of that, she liked to be hands-on with every aspect of her hotel. With a couple of extra hours she could catch up on some paperwork she had been procrastinating attending to.

With a sigh, she dragged herself up and stumbled to the bathroom to wash her face. Since she had a couple of hours she didn't have to get dressed yet, so she'd lounge around in her PJs a while longer. Maggie had her own little apartment up in the attic of the hotel, it had two bedrooms, two bathrooms, a small kitchen, and a living room, it wasn't lavish, but it was her home and she loved it.

Yawning as she walked into the living room, she sat down at the table and rubbed at her tired eyes. Being tired wasn't new to her, since she hated sleep she had survived on around five or six hours of sleep a night since she was a kid so she was used to that underlying sluggish feeling that went with never quite getting enough sleep.

Maggie was just opening her laptop when she smelled something.

Something burning maybe?

With a frown, she stood and walked to the kitchen, she didn't often cook, she wasn't great at it—grilled cheese sandwiches and salads were about all she could manage—so she usually just brought whatever was left in the kitchen at the end of the day home for dinner. She couldn't think of anything that should be burning in the kitchen, but nonetheless her feet seemed to have decided it was worthwhile to check.

As she pushed open the kitchen door she saw the room was dark, just as it should be.

When she turned back around to the living room she saw it.

Smoke.

Seeping under the door that led out to the hall where there was a small staircase leading down to the third floor of the hotel.

Was her hotel on fire?

"No, that's ridiculous," she berated herself aloud. "You're probably just dreaming." She put her fingers on her forearm and pinched herself. The sharp pain told her that she wasn't asleep.

This was real.

Her heart rate accelerated, and her breath wheezed in and out of her chest in short, sharp pants as she ran to her front door. Her fingers shook so badly it took her several attempts to undo the chain and then fling the door open.

That tiny sliver of hope that this still might be a dream was gone when she stood in the hall.

Smoke.

There was smoke everywhere.

It filled the hall and made her think of the Halloween party they'd had last year. The mayor had gone all out, they'd decorated the entire town, they'd had games and trick-or-treating, and a huge haunted house with smoke machines. It had creeped her out then, and this creeped her out so much more.

Coughing as the smoke immediately irritated her lungs, she pressed a hand over her mouth, knowing it would do little good, and stumbled through the haze to the top of the stairs.

Flames.

She could see the fire burning down there.

She was trapped.

The reality hit her like a ton of bricks, and she staggered backward into the wall, sliding down it to land with a thump on the smooth hardwood floor.

The fire had already reached the third floor, there was no way she could get through it to the front door. This was the attic, it wasn't like she could just jump out a window and run to safety.

This was it.

This was how she was going to die.

Fear like nothing else she had ever experienced—and she had a lot of practice with fear—crashed down on her. A sense of claustrophobia gnawed at her stomach, she'd never been trapped before, not like this anyway. There was nowhere to go, nothing she could do to save herself, and that left her feeling so helpless she almost considered trying to run through the flames.

But that would be suicide.

Choking on a sob, Maggie shoved back onto her feet, already feeling lightheaded from the smoke inhalation, and hurried down the hall as quickly as she could back to her apartment.

River's End was a small town, and even though the hotel was a mile south of the town someone would surely have seen the fire, or one of the guests would have called it in. Help would be coming, she just had to find a way to stay alive until it arrived.

Moving to her bathroom, her movements sluggish, she crawled into her shower, and taking the showerhead with her she pressed herself into the back corner. The water from the shower might hold off the flames if they reached her before the firefighters, but she was more worried about the smoke.

It was seeping into her apartment, filling it up, stealing all the oxygen, just like it would seep inside her lungs, filling them up and stealing all their oxygen.

Tears trickled from her stinging eyes, she coughed great big, angry coughs that tore at her throat, and waited for either death or rescue.

Maggie prayed it would be the latter.

~

3:53 A.M.

He wanted to throw something.

Preferably the phone that he held in his hand.

Had he not been at work there was a good chance that Theo Black would have followed through on that impulse and tossed his phone into the nearest wall, taking whatever satisfaction he could from shattering the device.

But he was at work, and smashing his phone would only lead to one of his colleagues wanting to know why he had done it. That would lead to questions he did not want to answer.

He'd returned to River's End with his tail between his legs, no longer the fun-loving, carefree man he used to be. He'd lost the woman he loved, not to death or disease, but to another man. It was petty and childish to be sulking about it—Theo knew that—and yet his heart had been shattered into a million pieces. She hadn't even known how he felt about her, she'd thought they were just friends, and then she'd met someone and fallen in love.

Theo had prayed it wouldn't work out.

How selfish was that?

That he would put his own happiness above hers, and yet that was how he felt.

Tonight's phone call—which he had cowardly let go to voicemail so he wouldn't have to talk to her—put any notion that she would break things off and come chasing after him to bed.

It was never going to happen.

The finality of it should give him closure, but it didn't.

Friends.

How he hated getting benched in the friend zone. It was the worst thing that could happen ...

Theo's train of thought trailed off when the siren sounded. It was time to roll. Theo wasn't the only one who stopped what they were doing and started moving, throwing on their gear and climbing into the truck, the rest of the team were there as well, moving with the practiced ease which came from doing this hundreds of times before.

"Where are we heading?" he asked, pleased to have something else to focus on instead of his love life—or lack thereof.

"Honeysuckle Hotel," came the curt reply from Timothy.

His heart dropped.

He knew why his friend was being curt, and it had nothing to do with his temper. Honeysuckle Hotel was owned and run by Maggie Wilson. Maggie had grown up in River's End, the hotel had been in her family for generations, and just like him, his team had also known her most of their lives.

Maggie was a friend, and he prayed that she had gotten out of the building in time. Even if she had, the loss of the hotel was going to be a devastating blow. As much as he loved his job, being a firefighter had been all he'd wanted to do when he'd left the Marines, that didn't mean he didn't have a healthy respect for fire and its power.

River's End wasn't a big town, and with lights flashing and sirens screaming it took only a few minutes before he could see the smoke and the flames illuminating the night.

It looked bad.

Everyone in the truck was tense.

It was early April, but it had been a mild winter, and the weather had started warming up in March, there had to be a couple of dozen people staying at the hotel. River's End was nestled just a little way up a mountain, in the winter people came to ski and snowboard, in the warmer weather they came to hike, camp, and ride bikes, or do water sports on the river. The Honeysuckle Hotel was the only hotel in town, although there were a few motels in nearby towns, and while they knew guests were staying there, there would be no way for them to know how many.

Which meant people might die.

If Maggie had somehow gotten out, she would be able to tell them how many people she had staying there.

But Maggie might not get out.

The truck pulled to a stop and Theo was out in seconds. People milled about, coughing and crying, ambulances and the cops would be on scene any minute, but right now, Theo's biggest concern was making sure everyone who had been in the hotel when the blaze started got out.

He scanned the crowd and immediately noticed Maggie's groundskeeper heading toward them. The older man lived in a small property down the back of the gardens, if anyone might know how many people were in the hotel it was him.

"Mr. Oaks," he called out, waving the man over. "Is Mags still in there?"

Worried brown eyes met his. "Yes."

His stomach dropped. Maggie lived in the attic, which had been converted into a small apartment, that was four floors up.

"How many guests were staying here?" he asked, already preparing to walk through the flames to find his friend. Maggie was a sweet woman, quiet but always in control, he'd known her since he and his family had moved to River's End after his dad retired from the military. He had been four when they'd moved here, Maggie had been only two, he remembered Christmas parties and Fourth of July's the town had celebrated out here at the hotel, and the little girl with the mop of brown curls that had been the heart of the town. Maggie was a sweetheart, and he *would* get her out of there.

"Forty-seven," Mr. Oaks replied.

Theo nodded, then turned to his team. "We need to find out how many people got out, there's forty-seven, forty-eight in total if we count Mags. I'm going up to the attic to search for her," he said, steeling himself for what was to come. It wouldn't be the first time he had walked through the flames to save someone, but it was the first time the stakes had been this high.

His team all sprang into action, and donning his helmet and self-contained breathing apparatus, Theo stepped inside the burning building.

The heat he was used to, the hazy orange glow that was a mixture of dancing flames and plumes of smoke he was also used to, but the hammering in his chest as he hurried as fast as he safely could up four flights of stairs wondering if with each step he took if he was going to be too late to save Maggie, that he wasn't used to.

Indecision gnawed at him. There was a chance that Maggie had been awakened by the flames and started to try to find safe passage through them and out of the hotel. She might not be in her apartment when he reached it, and by the time he backtracked and searched every room on each of the three floors, she would most likely be dead.

No.

He wouldn't let that happen.

Determinedly, he plowed onward, past the flames that were clinging to the building, devouring it piece by piece, until he reached the attic.

"Maggie?" he called out as he flung open her door.

A laptop sat open on the table, but there was no sign of Maggie anywhere.

"Maggie, it's Theo, can you hear me?" he yelled as he searched the kitchen and then moved onto the bedrooms.

There was no answer to his repeated calls, and he prayed that was because she had passed out and not because she was dead.

"Maggie," he said again, but this time it was a hissed whisper when he opened the bathroom door and saw her huddled in the corner of the shower. A wet towel covered her body, and her head lolled to the side at an awkward angle.

Dead?

Unconscious?

Yanking open the shower door, he dropped to his knees beside her. As he touched his fingertips to her neck he noticed the towel was still wet, and the showerhead rested on the floor beside her. She must have been conscious recently, dousing herself in water to try to keep the smoke—and the flames if they came near her—at bay.

"Please be alive, please be alive," he murmured as he pressed firmly on her neck in search of a pulse.

It took him a moment, but he found it.

A relieved breath whooshed out.

She was still alive, but they still had to get all the way back downstairs, and she'd already been in the smoke-filled building for longer than she should be.

"Maggie, honey, you hear me?" he asked, tapping at her cheek.

She groaned, coughed, and then her lashes fluttered against her pale cheeks. A moment later her eyes opened, and she looked at him, confusion written all over her pretty face.

"It's Theo," he told her, aware that she probably couldn't see his face through the smoke and his mask.

"Theo," she said on an exhale, it was all she could get out before she erupted into a coughing fit. Each harsh wheeze and shudder of her body only served to remind him that her time was running out.

"Hold on, sweetheart, I'm going to get you out of here," he promised, his fingers stroking her cheek in the hopes of soothing her.

Maggie opened her mouth but started coughing again, her eyes drooping closed even as she fought to keep them open.

"Just rest, don't try to talk, you keep breathing okay, don't give up on me, you got this," he assured her as he lifted her and draped her over his shoulders in a fireman's carry.

Fighting the urge to give Maggie his SCBA to ease the harsh breaths she was taking, the only reason he didn't give in to temptation was because he knew he was their only way out of here. He was a firefighter, trained to walk through burning buildings, Maggie ran a hotel, and her body was already weakened from the smoke. There was no way she was walking out of here on her own.

With his friend hanging limply across his shoulders, Theo began the trek back through the hotel and prayed Maggie would still be alive when he got them out.

~

4:07 A.M.

She wasn't really unconscious, and yet she wasn't really conscious either.

Maggie hung limply in her friend Theo's grasp as he walked through the fire.

The flames were everywhere, leaping above them, dancing about Theo's feet, reaching out as though they wanted to grab hold of them, drag them down, and consume them until they were nothing but dust.

She should be doing something.

She should be helping Theo.

At the very least she should be walking on her own two feet so he didn't have to carry her.

She tried to move, to speak, to tell him that he could put her down, but she found that she no longer had control over her own body.

It was like the two had become disconnected.

Her mind and her body were no longer one and the same. Her body hung across Theo's shoulders, and her mind floated somewhere above it.

The smoke stung her eyes and burned her throat. The heat was overwhelming and stole her breath every bit as much as the smoke did.

Maggie knew she was in bad shape.

It was getting harder and harder to draw air into her lungs.

She knew it was a combination of the lack of oxygen as the fire stole all that was left in the building, and the fact that her body was growing weaker by the second. If they didn't get out of here soon she was beginning to think she might not survive.

Theo was plodding steadily onward, but she had lost her bearings, full of dancing flames the hotel all looked the same and she couldn't figure out which floor they were on, and how much longer it would be until they finally reached the front door and escaped this burning hell.

She was going to die in here.

The reality of how precarious her situation was, hit her like a ton of bricks.

She was going to die.

Maggie knew she should probably be more upset about the idea, but in a way it was a relief. The lie she had told had weighed so heavily on her for most of her life, and she was so tired of lugging around that burden. Her penance was to spend her life alone, and escaping that would be a blessing.

Maybe she would finally find the relief she sought.

Or maybe she wouldn't.

Maybe whatever lay beyond this life would be worse.

She believed in Heaven and Hell, and given what she had done she certainly deserved to spend eternity being punished for it, so she would soon find herself in Hell.

The thought made her shudder, and as much as she fought to keep her eyes open, they felt like they were being weighed down with lead and closed against her will.

Blackness started to close in on her.

Tugging at the edges of her mind.

Trying to claim her.

Maggie was about to give in to it when all of a sudden, a blast of fresh air washed over her, ripping the last of the air from her lungs, and she burst into a violent coughing fit.

She felt herself be rearranged in Theo's arms so she was cradled against his chest instead of draped across his shoulders, and he started moving more quickly with her.

"I need EMTs now," he screamed.

His voice seemed to echo in her head.

She wanted to tell him that she was okay, that he didn't have to worry about her, but all she could do was shake in his arms and cough.

More people—paramedics she presumed—appeared beside her. Theo laid her down on a gurney and as soon as he let go of her the panic that had been dulled by the smoke slammed into her.

She'd nearly died.

And she knew enough about smoke inhalation to know that she still might.

She didn't want to be alone.

Maggie tried to find Theo, but her eyes were stinging and tearing up, and she couldn't see through them enough to find his face. She attempted to say his name but all that came out was more coughing. Her hand moved, seeking his even though it had no idea where to reach.

Then cool fingers closed around hers and a face leaned in close, a hand stroked her hair and Theo's voice spoke through the chaos, "It's okay, Mags, I'm right here, I'm not going anywhere, just rest and let the medics take care of you."

Doing as her friend instructed, Maggie let the feel of his hand holding hers center her and keep her secured in the commotion that buzzed around her. Medics put an oxygen mask on her, they put a pulse ox cable on one of her fingers, they started an IV, and covered her with a blanket.

Slowly the oxygen and whatever drugs they were giving her began to work their magic. She breathed a little easier, and the vicious headache assaulting her began to lessen. As the medics dealt with her physical symptoms from the smoke inhalation, the psychological and emotional ramifications of what had happened began to make themselves known.

There was no amount of drugs in the world that could dull that pain.

Theo was still beside her, still holding her hand, and she turned watery eyes from him to the burning hotel, and then back to her friend again. He had just saved her life, but there was nothing he could do to save her hotel or save her from the fallout.

This place had been in her family for generations, and she had let it burn down.

Reaching up with her free hand she tugged the oxygen mask down. "Is any of it going to survive?" she asked her firefighter friend.

"I don't know. I know it's hard but try not to worry about it now."

As if she could do anything but. Her eyes were no longer watering just because of the smoke, now there were tears as well. "Theo, you saved my life. How can I ever thank you for that?" she said, her voice hoarse. Talking irritated her throat and her lungs, but she needed him to know how much she appreciated what he had done for her.

"No need to thank me." He smiled down at her. "Just doing my job, and any one of the guys would have walked through that fire for you, sweetheart."

While she knew that was true it hadn't been any of the guys who had walked through the flames to get her out, it was Theo, and she would be eternally grateful. She shook her head, ignoring the way it jarred and restarted the headache. "You saved my life, and I won't ever forget that."

"You're going to make me blush, and if my ego gets any bigger then there won't be room for both of us in the ambulance," he teased.

"You're coming with me to the hospital?" Relief washed over her at the prospect, she didn't want to be alone right now.

"Of course, I wouldn't make you go alone. Now stop talking, and let's put this back on you." He released his grip on her hand for a moment to gently tug the oxygen mask from her hand and put it back on, adjusting the straps so it fitted snugly. Then before he took a seat beside her, he reached for her hand again.

That he was staying with her when she knew he must be itching to get back to putting out the fire that was destroying her hotel was touching.

She had known Theo Black and his family practically her entire life, and while he didn't know the details, he knew that she didn't really have any family. Maggie loved everyone in the town but fought hard to not let anyone get too close.

If Theo didn't go with her she would be alone, and that was the last thing she needed right now.

As good as she was at dealing with things on her own, for once it was nice to have someone there to lean on.

Just a little.

That the person she had to lean on was her big, strong, oozing reassurance friend was a bonus.

Okay, Theo was also the sexist guy she knew, not that she would ever tell him that or let herself think about it too much.

Thinking about things led to making bad decisions and she already knew what her penance was for her lies.

"Maggie, stop worrying, there's nothing we can do right now to change anything and the most important thing is that we got you out alive. So stop the wheels turning in that pretty little head of yours and just rest. You're going to be okay, and I'm going to be right here. Close your eyes, sweetheart, for now let's just focus on getting you well."

He was right.

There was nothing she could do about the fire right now, and she was tired.

So very tired.

Clutching Theo's hand as tightly as she could, she let exhaustion wash her away into unconsciousness.

~

3:28 P.M.

Maggie's chest rose and fell with each breath she took.

Theo sat in a chair beside her bed, still holding her hand because he wanted her to know the second she woke up that he'd kept his promise to stay with her so she wouldn't be alone.

Over the last twelve hours or so, she'd had chest x-rays and blood work done to determine how badly the smoke had affected her. She had managed to avoid being intubated, and while she still had the oxygen mask on, her doctor had said if she continued to improve, he'd change to a nose tube, and then if she continued to breathe well on her own she would be able to go home.

The relief that she was alive and was going to be okay hummed through his veins. If he hadn't gotten to her in time then Theo knew the guilt of being unable to save her would have stayed with him.

Walking through the flames with Maggie on his shoulders had seemed like the longest few minutes of his life. She'd been so still, a dead weight hanging off him, and while she was a tiny little thing and certainly didn't weigh much, the presence had been crushing because his friend's life rested solely in his hands. If he hadn't been able to get her out it would have been his fault. He'd been terrified that she was already gone and the hacking coughs that had ripped from her chest the second the fresh air hit her had been the most beautiful sound he'd ever heard.

"How's she doing?" he asked as the door to her room swung open, and her doctor strode through.

The man didn't reply, just strode calmly over to the bed, picked up Maggie's wrist to check her pulse, checked the monitors standing guard around her bed, listened to her chest with his stethoscope, and grabbed her chart to jot down some notes.

"If you don't say something soon I'm going to beat you up," he growled. Not only was the man Maggie's doctor, but he was also Theo's older brother.

"Calm down." Levi shot him a grin. "She's stable so you can stop worrying about her. And you know I'm your big brother, you can't beat me up."

Theo growled again because as many hours as he spent in the gym he knew his brother spent equally as much time there and they were evenly enough matched that beating him up wouldn't be a sure thing. But despite his brother's annoying calm his nerves did settle. Maggie was going to be okay, and that was all that mattered.

"Everyone made it out of the fire alive, we had a couple of smoke inhalation cases, milder than Maggie's, but thankfully everyone is going to be fine," Levi told him.

While he had gone up for Maggie his team had gotten the last of the guests out, and while he would have loved to stay and work on putting the fire out, he knew that Maggie didn't have family who could come and be with her. She was scared, she'd nearly died, she'd lost her business, he couldn't stand the thought of her being alone, so in the end it was an easy sacrifice to make. Friendship trumped work any day of the week.

"How long do you think she's going to be out?" he asked his brother. Maggie had passed out in the ambulance, and she hadn't regained consciousness yet, he wasn't sure if it was as a result of the smoke or whatever drugs were dripping into the back of her hand through her IV.

"She could wake up at any time, she really is okay, Theo," Levi assured him. Everyone in River's End cared about Maggie, she was just the sweetest thing, and he knew that she'd had a rough childhood and tended to keep to herself. He knew that her parents had abused drugs and alcohol, her dad eventually going to prison, and she'd gone to live with her grandparents. She had a brother, but she didn't appear to be close with him, and since she didn't let any of her friends get too close she was a bit of a mystery.

As if to prove his brother's point, Maggie groaned, her eyelashes fluttering on her milky white cheeks. Theo stood so that he'd be the first thing she saw when she opened her eyes.

"Hey, sweetheart," he crooned, stroking her wavy brown locks. "You're in the hospital, Levi's here, he's taking good care of you, and you know I'd beat him up if he wasn't."

A small smile quirked her lips up and she squeezed his hand. "My head hurts, my chest too," she murmured.

"Yeah, you're going to hurt for a while," Levi told her. "But your vitals are all improving, and if you keep doing well then you can go home tomorrow."

Maggie reached up and pulled the oxygen mask away from her face. "How long have I been here?"

"Almost twelve hours," he replied.

Shock filtered through her eyes and then she steeled herself and met his gaze directly. "Did anyone die in the fire?"

"No," he assured her. "Everyone got out, there were a few more smoke inhalation cases but yours was the most serious."

She absorbed this, but the tense lines on her forehead didn't ease. "How bad was the damage? Is the fire out? Did it destroy everything?"

Her voice was hoarse, and she had to pause between each sentence to cough. His protective instincts told him to filter his answers so as not to cause her more stress, but that wasn't going to help her in the long run. Besides, this was Maggie they were talking about, he'd served in the military before becoming a firefighter and he'd never seen anyone with greater self-control than her. "The guys called, the fire is out, the damage is bad but not as bad as it could have been. I'll help you organize someone to come out and inspect the building as soon as we clear it, then you can find out how quickly you'll be back in business."

Her beautiful big eyes grew watery, and in this moment he would do anything it took to make her feel better. "But it's going to take a few months at least to get the place rebuilt. I'll have to replace all the furnishings. Whatever wasn't destroyed by the fire, the water would have ruined. And all of my things," she swallowed audibly, then choked on a sob before erupting into another coughing fit.

Levi pried the oxygen mask from her hand and fitted it back on her face while Theo stroked his thumb across her knuckles. "We'll work it out, Maggie. You know everyone in River's End will do anything they can to help you get back up and running again. Until you do you can stay with me."

Her eyes flew to his. "What?" she murmured through the mask.

"You have to stay someplace, and we're friends, my house is big enough that you'll still have your own space if you need it, but you won't be alone. And you're going to need to have someone monitor you when you get out of here anyway, right, Levi?" He turned to his brother for backup. He didn't want Maggie to be alone when she left here, she needed support right now, and they were friends, he could be there for her.

"That's right," Levi agreed. "Smoke inhalation can get worse after a time, so yes, when I discharge you you're going to need to be observed for at least the next twenty-four hours or so, so staying with Theo would solve both problems."

"What do you say, want to be my roommate for a while?" he asked.

Tears trickled down her cheeks, and she pulled the oxygen mask away again. "You'd really let me stay with you?"

"Of course," he replied, brushing away her tears. "What are friends for?"

"This is really your day, huh, Black?" She gave him a weak smile. "You saved my life and you're letting me stay with you. That ego of yours is going to get even bigger."

"You know it." He grinned.

"Now that we have that settled would you please leave this on." Levi sounded exasperated as he re-fitted the mask over her face. "If you want to go home tomorrow then you need more rest, and oxygen. If you keep doing well we'll move to the nose tube soon, and you can be free of this mask."

"Levi is right, you get some rest."

"You can leave if you want, you don't have to stay." Maggie said the words but her eyes told a different story. She was usually so strong, she kept herself all calm and in control, but everything that had happened tonight had knocked down her barriers, for a time at least.

"I'm not going anywhere," he promised, resuming his spot in the chair at her bedside. "Now, listen to your doctor and close those pretty eyes of yours and go to sleep."

In less than a minute her hand went limp in his and her breathing evened out as she drifted off to sleep leaving him to keep vigil over her sleeping form.

April 6th
5:40 A.M.

"You couldn't have waited until the sun came up at least?" Theo asked as he drove them through the quiet early morning.

"I couldn't stay in the hospital a second longer," Maggie told him. Her throat was still scratchy, her lungs still felt like they were clogged with smoke, her eyes were puffy and itchy, and a headache still pounded at her temples, but she was well and truly ready to be out of the hospital.

She had to start preparing to get her hotel back in business.

As soon as the sun was up she was going to ask Theo if he could take her over to the hotel, she had to see for herself just how bad things were. Then once she knew that, she would start approaching builders and collecting estimates. If the damage wasn't too bad then maybe she could be up and running—at least partially—before the summer peak. It was a long shot, but it was all she really had. The hotel was her life, it was her home and her business, and an important part of her family, she *would* do whatever it took to get back in business as soon as she possibly could.

"I understand that, I do, but I worry about you." Theo took his eyes off the road to glance over at her.

"I know you do." She smiled at him. He had been amazing through these last twenty-four hours, and not just the whole walking through fire to save her and offering to share his home with her. He'd sat by her bed, holding her hand, for hours, and that meant the most to her.

She was so used to being on her own, keeping people—even her friends—at a distance, but the fire had stripped away her defenses, and she'd been scared and desperate for someone to be there, and Theo had been. She wasn't used to relying on anyone else, and she thought it should feel strange to be leaning on him, but for some reason it didn't.

"Thanks, Theo," she said, reaching over and resting her hand on his arm.

"You don't have to keep thanking me, Mags," he reminded her, patting her hand before returning his to the steering wheel.

"Of course I do, you saved my life, you stayed with me in the hospital, you're letting me stay with you, I could say thank you a hundred times a day, every day for the rest of my life, and it wouldn't be enough."

"Remember my ego, sweetheart." He laughed.

She giggled back. Despite all his talk about his ego, one of the great things about Theo Black was that he didn't have one. He was sexy as can be with dark hair, hazel eyes, and a body women drooled over, he had a few tattoos, a winning smile, and he was easygoing and fun to be around, not to mention the fact that he saved people for a living.

He was basically perfect.

Heat pooled in her stomach and before she realized it, Maggie was imagining what it would be like to have his huge hands wrapped around her waist, dragging her up against his rock hard chest. His mouth would be hot against hers, as he'd kiss her passionately, then he'd rip her clothes off and bury himself deep inside her, taking them both to the edge of unbridled passion and then tumbling over it.

"Mags, you okay? You just went bright red. Do you need me to turn around, take you back to the hospital?"

"What?" She blinked and realized she must have been blushing at her little daydream. "Oh, yeah, fine," she said, embarrassed.

What was she doing?

Daydreaming about sex with Theo was a bad idea.

He was her friend, and she didn't want to lose him over one night of uncontrollable libido.

"Wait till I come round and get you in case you're still a little unsteady on your feet," he ordered as he parked his car in his driveway.

She should push all thoughts of kissing and making out from her mind, but when he opened her door for her and his large hand closed gently around her forearm as he helped her climb down out of his truck, her libido skyrocketed.

She wanted to kiss Theo.

She wanted to do a whole lot more than kiss Theo.

"I'll give you some of my old sweatpants and a t-shirt to wear today, and tomorrow you can go shopping and get some new clothes, you can borrow my credit card, pay me back once you get things sorted out."

Maggie was barely listening to him as they walked toward his front door, all she could think about was what his lips would feel like on hers. And what they would feel like on certain other body parts.

He opened the door and guided her inside, flipping on the lights, and like a switch had been flipped inside her she reached up, curled her arms around his neck, stood on her tiptoes, and kissed him.

For a second, all her problems slipped away as he kissed her back, but then his hands closed over her shoulders, and he gently pushed her away. "Maggie, what are you doing?"

"Kissing you," she replied, trying not to feel hurt that he'd rebuffed her. What had she expected him to do? He'd just pulled her from a fire and spent the last twenty-four hours sitting at her hospital bedside, of course he didn't want to have sex with her.

"Mags," he said, his voice impossibly gentle, "you can't even take a breath without wincing in pain, and Levi said you're going to find yourself getting breathless after even a little exertion for the next few days. Besides, you've just endured an emotional trauma, I don't think you really know what you're doing."

"I know exactly what I'm doing," she countered and kissed him again, more passionately this time, trying to convey just how much she needed this.

"Maggie," he murmured when she ended the kiss.

She cut him off with another kiss, her fingers fumbling with the buttons of his shirt.

"Stop," he said, catching both of her hands in one of his, stilling their near frantic attempts to undress him. "We can't do this. *I* can't do this, it would be taking advantage of you while you're vulnerable."

"I'm a big girl. I need this, Theo, please, make me forget about everything that happened, just for a few minutes," she begged. She hated to beg, hated for him to see her vulnerable like this, but she needed a connection to another human being, just for one precious moment. She was so tired of being alone, she was so tired of the guilt that was always threatening to crush her, she was so tired of trying to pretend that everything was okay all the time. For just a second she wanted to forget all about it.

Theo groaned, and she was sure he was going to say no when he snatched her up into his arms and took the stairs two at a time.

In his bedroom, he lay her down, and his eyes met hers for a brief moment, seeking assurance that this was really what she wanted. When she nodded, he grabbed hold of the scrubs that the hospital had given her to wear and pulled them down her legs, tossing them onto the floor.

She didn't have any underwear on, so she was naked from the waist down, she might have felt embarrassed if it wasn't for the look on his face.

He looked like he wanted to devour her.

"Last chance to back out, sweetheart," he said as he spread her legs and settled himself between them.

"I'm not backing out." She arched a challenging brow at him. For now she was throwing caution to the wind, she was letting go of everything, she was setting everything aside, her problems would still be there later, but for now, she was just going to be.

His fingertips trailed up and down her inner thigh, working their way closer to the spot that screamed for his attention. His lips followed the path his fingers had taken, kissing and licking his way toward her center.

"Get ready to forget everything, including your own name," he told her with a wicked grin right before his mouth claimed her.

Maggie moaned, her fingers curling into the quilt as his tongue began to ravish her.

She'd never felt anything like this before.

She'd been with very few men in her life, her high school boyfriend because she'd felt pressured to sleep with him, and her college boyfriend for the same reason, but nothing they had done had made her feel like this.

His mouth with that magic tongue was working her higher and higher.

Sensations began to flood through her system.

It was like she had been filled with some sort of liquid magic that was now moving through her veins, consuming every part of her.

"Theo," she panted as he slid his fingers inside her, stroking deep.

"Let go, Maggie, let go of everything but this moment, don't think, just feel," he told her. Then his mouth claimed her, his tongue swirled, and the feelings inside her swelled to overflowing.

Her natural inclination was to fight against it, to fight against anything that would bring her even an iota of happiness, but Theo didn't let up. His tongue continued to tease her, his fingers continued to stroke her, and she finally allowed herself to let go.

The explosion that burst inside her took her breath away.

She screamed as she came on a wave of emotion and intense bliss that seemed to go on forever.

She couldn't see, couldn't hear, couldn't move, couldn't even think. All she could do was feel.

When she slowly floated back down to earth the first thing she saw was Theo standing over her, a smug look on his gorgeous face. "Need me to remind you of your name?"

"Oh yeah," she murmured.

"Ready for round two?" he asked as he undid the buckle on his jeans.

"Oh yeah." She nodded.

"Good because that was nothing compared to how good this is going to be." He smirked as he slid his jeans down his muscled legs. "By the time I'm done with you, you're going to have forgotten my name as well."

"That would never happen," she said as she watched him shed his boxers and sheath himself with a condom. There was no way she could ever forget everything that Theo had done for her.

He was her hero.

"We'll see." He winked as he thrust into her in one smooth motion.

She gasped at the size of him and the way he stretched her, but he was already moving, and although she'd thought there was no way her sated body could do anything but just lie there, she wrapped her legs around him, drawing him further into her body as she met him thrust for thrust.

Her hero was about to make magic happen again.

~

9:54 A.M.

Maggie was in his bed.

That was the first thought that crossed Theo's mind when he woke up.

What had he been thinking?

Sex with Maggie had to be one of the stupidest things he had ever done.

With a groan, he carefully slid out of bed, careful not to disturb Maggie, who had draped her naked body across his in her sleep. She needed the rest, and he needed not to talk to her just yet.

He had to decide how to handle this.

And quickly.

He'd invited Maggie to stay here so he was going to be seeing her every day until her hotel was fixed and she moved back home, and he didn't want things to be awkward between them.

Didn't want things to be awkward between them?

He balked at his stupidity. It was a little late to be worrying about that.

Out of bed, he grabbed his jeans, a clean pair of boxers, and a t-shirt, and then laid out some clothes for Maggie to wear when she woke up.

Going into his bathroom, he splashed some cold water on his face as though that could wash away what he'd done.

If only it was that simple.

Last night was a mistake.

Theo knew better than most that sex between friends was never a good idea. It never worked out, both parties always walked away unhappy, and he didn't want that for Maggie.

Leaving the bathroom, he headed down to the kitchen, he should make something for Maggie to eat when she got up. She hadn't eaten yesterday at the hospital and he had taken responsibility for her when he'd asked her to stay with him. Instead of three rounds of mind-blowing sex, he should have brought her up to the spare bedroom, tucked her in, made sure she was comfortable, offered her something to eat, and then let her get the rest she so badly needed.

But he hadn't done that.

Instead, he had used Maggie.

She was beautiful, with delicate features, big chestnut brown eyes, and silky chocolate brown hair that tumbled down her back in a mass of thick waves. She was sweet and kind to everyone, her big heart was always ready to help someone in need. She didn't deserve what he had done to her.

He'd used her.

Used her to get a certain blonde-haired, blue-eyed someone out of his head.

Maggie was the exact opposite of his tornado.

No.

Not *his* tornado.

Amethyst Hatcher would never be his. She was married to someone else, and according to the phone message she'd left him yesterday, she was pregnant with her husband's baby. She had a family of her own now, she didn't see him as anything but a friend, and nothing was ever going to change that.

Theo knew he had to let it go, allowing himself to be consumed with love for a woman that didn't return his feelings was only going to leave him alone and sour forever.

When Maggie had kissed him last night he had kissed her back, intending the kiss to comfort and soothe her after the rotten day she'd had. But then she'd deepened the kiss, started trying to take his clothes off, and he'd lost his mind. He'd made her come with his mouth, his hands, and hot and heavy sex, and as amazing as it had been he knew it was a mistake.

Not that he was blaming Maggie.

She might have instigated things, but she'd been vulnerable and hurt and just lost everything. He'd done the one thing he thought he would never do, he'd taken advantage of a woman.

"That's not true."

He spun around from the stove where he was making bacon and eggs and pancakes for breakfast to find Maggie standing in the kitchen doorway. Ridiculous as it was, she looked even sexier in his sweatpants that she'd had to roll up several times so she didn't trip on them, and the t-shirt that was more like a dress on her, than she had in the hundred dollar dress she'd worn to his brother's engagement party last month.

She was stunning, but that didn't change the facts.

Last night was a mistake and one that he couldn't make again.

"What's not true?" he asked, sure that he hadn't said anything out loud so aiming for nonchalance but fearing he was failing miserably.

"You didn't take advantage of me last night. You're a good guy and you would never do that. I wanted what we did last night, no I needed it, you gave me one moment where I could forget about everything that happened, actually you gave me more than one moment, and that means everything to me."

She was so earnest, her eyes scrunched at the corners, too worried about him hating himself for what he had done to even realize what it exactly was that he had done.

Despite what Maggie thought, he *had* taken advantage of her. She'd nearly died and she'd lost everything, she had been vulnerable last night, and he'd used her to try to get Amethyst Hatcher out of his head.

"Thank you for saying that, but the facts are that what we did last night we shouldn't have done, it was a mistake, and we can't do it again," he told her. Although he said the words—and meant them—he felt a pang in his chest, like he had just lost something.

He prayed it wasn't Maggie.

He didn't want to lose one of his friends over one stupid moment of weakness. He hadn't slept in over twenty-four hours, he'd been riding a wave of adrenalin, and Maggie's sweet begging had gotten to him.

But he wouldn't allow it to happen again.

"That won't ever happen again," he repeated.

"Of course," she agreed quickly.

Too quickly.

For a moment he wondered—with a dose of horror—if Maggie wanted more. They'd been friends for so long and she'd never indicated that she wanted anything more than friendship from him. But what if that had been an act? What if she did want them to be a couple?

If Maggie had been hoping that something more was going to develop between them, if she'd thought there was more to it than just sex, then he was never going to forgive himself.

Today just kept getting worse and worse.

Maybe he should have taken her to the bed in the spare bedroom after they'd had sex so she didn't get the wrong idea. Instead, he had let her fall asleep in his arms, and now he was afraid that he had led her on.

"You making breakfast?" she asked. She'd schooled her features into an impenetrable mask that he couldn't see through, and dropped into a chair at his kitchen table.

"Yep, bacon, eggs, pancakes," he said, maybe he'd read her wrong before, maybe what they'd done had meant the same thing to her as it meant to him. Just sex. One friend helping out another, helping them forget the mess they'd found themselves in, and maybe that friend getting a little something out of it in return. And he had to admit that worrying about ruining his friendship with Maggie had certainly pushed thoughts of Amethyst and her husband and pregnancy to the back of his mind.

"Great, I'm starving."

"Then eat up, I made plenty," he told her, dishing her up a plate and setting it down in front of her.

"You got any juice?"

"You don't want to ask that question," he said with a grin as things between them settled back into the easy friendship they'd always had. "I've got apple juice, orange juice, mango juice, pineapple juice, guava juice, passionfruit, berry, and probably a couple I'm forgetting."

Maggie smiled. "Guava juice sounds amazing, I've never had that before."

"You're going to love it," he told her, going to the fridge and pouring her a glass before joining her at the table.

"So, what are your plans today?" she asked, taking a big bite of pancake. "Wow, this is delicious. So fluffy and soft, how did I not know that you're such a good cook?"

"I try to keep it secret otherwise the guys at the station would have me cooking for all of them every day."

"Your secret is safe with me." She winked.

Darn if she didn't look even sexier when she winked. "So," he cleared his throat, "plans for today. Well, the guys texted to say that the site will be secured by tomorrow so I thought I'd help you check out builders, see if we can set up some appointments for this week. I think it would be smart to get at least three quotes before you decide on who you want to use to rebuild. Unless you have someone in mind."

"There was a guy who redid some bathrooms for me a couple of years ago, he was good, but I don't even know if he's still in business, or if he'd be available at short notice. I need to get things moving as quickly as possible, I really don't want to have to miss the whole summer season, so depending on how bad things are, I'm hoping we might be able to be up and running by the Fourth of July."

Since he hadn't seen the extent of the damage, having spent the day in the hospital with Maggie, he didn't know if she was being optimistic or not. "Here's hoping. I'm not on shift again until tomorrow, so until then consider me all yours."

The words were out of his mouth before he even realized how they sounded.

Quickly he glanced at Maggie to see if she'd misinterpreted what he'd said.

He'd meant he was here to help her make phone calls, or go shopping, or anything else she needed, not that he was available for more bedroom action.

But Maggie was busy devouring breakfast and didn't spare a glance his way, so he guessed she'd taken it as he'd meant it.

That was good.

So why did he feel another pang in his chest?

10:36 A.M.

What had she been thinking?

She wasn't thinking.

That was all there was to it.

She had been emotional from everything that had happened and everything that had almost happened, and now she might have ruined a great friendship.

All because she had gone sex crazy.

Maggie didn't do random sex with random guys.

Okay, so Theo was hardly a random guy, he was a friend she had known since she was two years old, but just because she'd known him her whole life, and just because he had saved her life, didn't mean that the two of them should have had sex.

And they shouldn't have.

It should never have happened.

And yet ...

She wouldn't take it back even if she could.

But it was clear that Theo would.

He regretted what had happened between them.

What had been the most amazing, earth-shattering thing that had ever happened to her, to the guy she had done it with it was something he wished that he could take back.

Theo thought that it was a mistake.

A mistake he wished he could undo.

But it was out there now, and it was going to ruin everything unless they were careful.

And she really didn't want that to happen.

Theo was an important part of her life, and she wasn't going to lose him because she had let her emotions get the best of her and she'd acted on them in an inappropriate and uncharacteristic manner.

Even if Theo hadn't regretted them having sex it wouldn't really change anything. She didn't date. Being alone was her penance for lying and getting someone killed.

That lie—that felt like a million years ago—had led to the death of someone she had loved. What right did she have to live a happy life after that?

There was never going to be anything between her and Theo so why was she tying herself up in knots about it?

Even if she was looking for a relationship, Theo wasn't. He was still hung up on Amethyst Hatcher. She'd been a firefighter on his team before he'd moved back to River's End. Although she had never outright asked him about it, rumor around town was that Amethyst had gotten married to someone else, and nursing a broken heart, Theo had come slinking back here because he couldn't stand seeing the woman he loved with another man.

Theo didn't just not want her, he didn't want any woman, so this whole thing was pointless.

She should stop thinking about it.

She should stop replaying that mind-blowing sex in her head.

She should stop being hurt because he had brushed off what had happened between them like it was no big deal.

But she *was* hurt.

It was stupid, it was ridiculous, it was the most ludicrous thing she had ever felt. She wasn't looking for a relationship, and neither was Theo, so no harm no foul, they should just pretend that it never happened and let their friendship go back to the way it was before.

Only she wasn't sure she could do it.

For her, something had changed last night.

Theo hadn't just given her orgasm after orgasm he had touched her heart, her soul, he had made her feel loved, special, cherished. Her family had been a mess when she was a kid, alcoholic father, drug addict mother, they hadn't cared about her, but her grandparents had. She was twelve when she had gone to live with them, and they had given her everything that her parents hadn't. She knew what it was like to feel loved and wanted, but no one had ever made her feel what Theo had.

It was something special, and everything inside of her screamed to grab hold of it and never let it go.

But that would mean abandoning her self-imposed punishment.

That wasn't something she could do.

"Argh," she groaned aloud, annoyed with herself. She had way bigger problems right now than that she appeared to be developing feelings for her friend. Her business and her home had burned down, she had insurance companies to deal with and builders to find, more than enough to keep her occupied until these feelings faded away.

And they would fade.

Right?

They had to.

The doorbell rang, and she pushed herself off the couch where she had been huddled, needing a little longer to hide before she could face the real world again.

"Hi, Meadow," she greeted her friend when she opened Theo's front door.

"Are you okay?" Meadow demanded, grabbing hold of her and dragging her into a fierce hug.

"I'm fine. A bit of a headache, tired, and my chest and throat hurt, but I'm lucky to be alive. I'm afraid you're going to be out of work for a while," she told her friend who worked as a chef in the restaurant of the hotel.

"That's not a problem." Meadow waved a dismissive hand. "I'm going to be out on maternity leave soon anyway."

"Yeah you are," she agreed, then couldn't stop a small shudder rippling through her.

"Come on, let's get you inside, you should be resting." Meadow ushered her into the house and closed the door behind them, then guided her over to the couch, pushing her gently onto it and then staring at her. "I'm so glad Theo got to you in time."

"That makes two of us," she said as she flopped back down against the couch cushions.

"That makes a whole town of us," Meadow corrected, easing her seven months pregnant body down to sit beside her. Although you couldn't tell by looking at her, Meadow was still recovering from the injuries she had sustained running from her kidnapper, she was supposed to be taking it easy, but that wasn't Meadow. "Everyone would have been devastated if anything had happened to you."

That was both true and untrue.

Given everything that her grandparents had done for this town, she had inadvertently become the town sweetheart, but she also kept everyone at a distance. It was the way it had to be. If she let anyone get too close, they might figure out her lie and its consequences, and then no one would want to be close to her anyway.

It was exhausting keeping up this front all the time, but it was the way it had to be.

It was the cost of her lie.

Loneliness and nightmares.

Nightmares.

With a start, she realized that last night was the first time ever that bad dreams hadn't plagued her sleep.

Theo.

It was his warm body beside hers, his arms wrapped snuggly around her, his comforting presence that must have eased her subconscious and allowed it to finally let go. It was nice, but she knew that it would never happen again.

"Maggie?"

"What?" She'd forgotten Meadow was here.

"Where's Theo?"

"Oh, I needed clothes, but I wasn't ready to go to the store dressed like this so I asked him to go and pick up some things for me."

"That's so sweet of him. Theo is such a great guy, it's such a shame that he can't get over Amethyst Hatcher and find happiness of his own," Meadow said with a dreamy look on her face.

Meadow had recently found that elusive happiness.

Just two months ago Meadow had arrived, pregnant and homeless, in River's End. Running from a monster, she'd come face to face with a man who would end up changing the course of her life.

Abe Black.

Town sheriff, self-confirmed bachelor, Theo's older brother, and Meadow's savior.

Now Meadow and Abe were engaged, he was committed to helping her raise her baby, and they were planning the rest of their lives.

Meadow had been through so much, more than most people could even imagine, and yet she had come through it all like a star. She was positive and bubbly, friends already with everyone in this close-knit little town, she was like a ray of sunshine. Maggie knew that she still struggled, that she was still vulnerable underneath the bright exterior. She was uncomfortable with anyone touching her if she hadn't initiated, she was liable to panic if you appeared behind her unannounced, and she still had nightmares and unresolved issues. Still despite it all, Meadow was so strong.

So much stronger than she could ever hope to be.

"Maggie?" Meadow rested a concerned hand on her knee. "What's going on?"

Even though she had known Meadow the least amount of time of all of her friends they were probably the closest. It was because they had a shared trauma in their past. They had both suffered abuse, and although she had never told Meadow the details, she knew more than anyone else did.

"Theo and I had sex last night," she blurted out. She had no idea why, the words were just out before she even thought about it.

"You had what?" Meadow exclaimed.

"You heard me."

"He came onto you after everything that happened?" Meadow looked incredulous.

"No, uh, I came onto him." Maggie fixed her gaze on her hands which she had twisted in her lap.

"Eek, that's awesome." Meadow grinned. "If you two got together then we'd be sisters-in-law. How cool would that be?"

Unable to stop a smile from gracing her lips at Meadow's enthusiasm, it quickly faded away. "Only one problem with that. Theo is hung up on Amethyst."

"Make that two problems," Meadow corrected. "Theo is hung up on Amethyst, and you don't date."

She conceded that with a nod. She was a coward, she was hiding from happiness because she thought she deserved to be punished, but Meadow had been through hell, and it had only cemented her determination to find happiness and wrap both hands around it, clinging to it with all her might.

That was the difference between them. Meadow had experienced trauma, and it had made her want to find the good in the world. She had experienced trauma, and it had made her think the entire world was bad and that she was the worst.

Sometimes she wished that she might find a happy ending herself one day, but the reality was that that wasn't in the cards for her.

~

12:44 P.M.

"Is that everyone?" Sheriff Abe Black asked his deputy—and cousin—Julian.

"Yep, that was the last one," Julian replied as he wrote the final name on the whiteboard.

"All right." Abe nodded. "We'll have to go through each person one by one and see what we can come up with. For now, let's set aside Maggie, I know she's the most likely target given that it's her hotel, but we need to also look at the possibility that it was one of the guests." The idea that sweet little Maggie Wilson was the target of whoever had set fire to the Honeysuckle Hotel didn't sit well with him. Okay, he knew that she wasn't little Maggie Wilson anymore, but he was eight years older than her, and to him she would always be the sweet little girl with the long wavy brown locks and those big innocent eyes. He knew about the rough childhood she'd had, and he was glad that she'd had grandparents to take her in when her parents went to prison, but she'd been through enough, and he didn't like the notion that someone was out to hurt her.

"We should also set Rosemary Trent to the side for now as well," Julian pointed out. "She's the other River's End resident, and she doesn't live at the hotel so it would be unlikely that anyone who wanted to hurt her would hurt her while she was at work."

Abe agreed with that assessment. If anyone was going to go after the woman who worked at the hotel front desk it would most likely be at her home. Not that he could see anyone wanting to hurt Rosemary Trent. The woman was almost seventy, had been a widow since she was in her twenties, raised three kids on her own, and was now the proud grandmother of ten, including a brand new baby boy. She'd lived in River's End her entire life and everyone loved her, there was no reason he could think of that she would be the target.

Not that he could think of any reason Maggie would be the target either.

Although the woman was a bit of an enigma.

Maggie had lived in River's End all her life as well, and she was widely accepted as the town sweetheart, everyone loved her, and while everyone knew her, he didn't know a single person who knew her really well. In fact the person who was probably closest with her was his fiancée, and while it would certainly make his job easier to pump Meadow for information on Maggie, he would never put the woman he loved in that position.

"All right, well, with Maggie and Rosemary out of the equation for the time being, we have forty-six other people who could have been the target of whoever set the hotel on fire," he said. When they'd gotten confirmation from the fire inspector that an accelerant had been used, meaning they were looking at a deliberate act and not a faulty appliance or accident, he and his deputies had started compiling a list of all the people who had been inside the hotel at the time the fire was lit so they could find the intended target. The holidaying families had all been set up at a motel just a couple of miles outside of town, contact information had been gathered, and they would speak with them as necessary.

"Six couples, two families of five, two families of four, a family of three, a family of six, and a group of seven friends," Julian said, pointing to each of their groups on the whiteboard.

"We've run basic criminal background checks on each of them, and only one name popped. One in the group of seven friends has a rap sheet for possession of drugs. Nothing major, and nothing recent, Josh

Majors is twenty-eight, and his last arrest was when he was twenty-one. It seems a bit of a stretch to believe that someone from seven years ago suddenly decided to come and take him out in a fire along with forty-seven other innocent people."

"This whole thing is a stretch." Julian sighed.

Abe was inclined to agree.

Targeting someone in a hotel along with nearly fifty other people didn't seem like the kind of thing someone would do. It was too risky, and unless they were looking at some kind of sociopath who was cold-blooded enough to take out innocent people who had nothing to do with his target, it didn't seem like the route anyone would take.

"Abe, I know none of us wants to think this, but the most logical target is Maggie. It's her hotel, so not only would it potentially take her out, but also destroy her home and her business. Plus she was on the fourth floor, up in the attic, so the chances of her getting out alive were the slimmest."

"I'm not disagreeing with you, but we know Maggie, and none of us know of anyone who would do this to her, so let's focus on our unknowns first and then we'll go and speak with Mags."

"All right. Well, as I said, we only have the one person with a criminal record, of course it's possible someone else is into something illegal and hasn't been caught for it yet. There's also one of the families, the McCoys," Julian said, tapping the photo of the family of six.

"What do we know about them?"

"The family is a blended one. He's a widow with two kids, she's divorced with a kid, and they just had a baby together. From what we've been able to see, she had to take out a restraining order on the ex-husband. He was harassing her, angry he lost custody of his son, angry that she had moved on, angry that Bill McCoy was playing dad to his kid, and especially angry that there was a new baby in the mix. He wouldn't leave the family alone, and he'd made an attempt to kidnap his son. If he thought he could scare the family out into the open with the fire, I guess it's possible he hoped in the ensuing commotion that he could snatch the kid and run."

Julian didn't sound convinced by the idea and he wasn't either, but nonetheless they would do their job and look into the family and the ex-husband to see if he could have been involved. "Anyone else have anything we should be looking into?"

"Well, one of the couples is wealthy, so there's always a chance that someone might have tried to do a kidnap for ransom only it didn't pan out," Julian replied.

Another possibility.

Another possibility he wasn't feeling.

"What else?"

"One of the other couples, the woman is a defense lawyer, they make enemies every time they turn around, she should be on our list as well. We'll look through all of her recent cases, look for any victims or victims' families who might be angry she got their assailant off. We'll also look at any disgruntled clients who wound up in prison, they could have sent someone to eliminate the lawyer."

Abe scrubbed his hands over his face, the more they looked at the guests in the hotel, the more he believed that this was about Maggie. But so far they had no proof of that. It could still just as easily be any of the people who were in there last night.

Only, if you wanted to kill someone—or even to scare them—then why would you go after them when they were on vacation and staying in a hotel?

Wouldn't it make more sense to go after them when they were in their own home, where you had more control over the situation?

Or perhaps that was the whole point.

Right now, they felt like they were spinning, no solid lead to jump on and pursue. The man—or woman—who had started the fire might have hoped that there would be so many potential victims that the real intended victim would get lost in the shuffle and they would be able to blend in and go unnoticed, no one would be looking for them because the cops had never correctly identified the target.

"Here's something," Julian began thoughtfully.

"Yeah?" he prompted.

"One of the families of four, the Hattocks. Middle-aged couple, two teenage children, a boy and a girl, both are foster kids. It looks like the boy has been getting into trouble at school recently."

"What kind of trouble?" Abe asked, his interest piqued.

"Trouble at school, failing grades, fights with other students, even a fight with a teacher, and fire starting. There have been some in his neighborhood, mostly cars and dumpsters, but a couple at his school, and even one at his house."

Fire starting.

Now that *was* interesting.

"We assumed that it was someone outside the hotel who set the fire, but if it was one of the guests that would be the perfect cover," Abe said. "He sneaks out, dumps the accelerant, then sets the fire, sneaks back in and then comes out along with everyone else. It's the perfect cover because we're not looking at anyone who was in the hotel as a suspect. This kid just jumped to the top of our suspect list," Abe declared.

Right now, he was happy with any direction that led away from Maggie, but he also wanted to get this man off the street. They'd lucked out that no one had died in the hotel fire, but that didn't mean they would be so lucky next time.

River's End was his town, he was the sheriff, and he took that responsibility seriously, even more so since he had fallen in love. He was going to be married this summer, and he was the father of Meadow's baby, even if he didn't share its DNA, he would die for that baby or Meadow. Those protective instincts reached out to everyone in this town, and he didn't care for someone messing with what was his.

If this fire starting kid was the one who had messed with his town then the kid would wind up where he belonged.

Behind bars.

~

3:12 P.M.

He was feeling quite satisfied with himself.

He had been planning this for a long time, and it was such a relief that everything had gone off without a hitch.

There had been so many things that could have gone wrong. The hotel had had more people in it than he'd thought it would, given the time of year. In hindsight, perhaps he should have expected the place to be busier. This town had tourists using the mountain all year round, so even in this lull between winter activities and summer ones the town appeared busy.

When he'd realized that there were so many people there and that the risks would be amped up he had nearly backed out. It wasn't like you could douse a building with a couple of hundred rooms in it in a couple of seconds.

Knowing that he could be caught, knowing that he could be arrested, knowing that all his secrets could come tumbling out, it was a lot of pressure and it would have been so much easier to walk away, choose a different time, it wasn't like it was a now or never kind of situation.

But he had never backed out on anything in his life, and he wasn't about to start now.

He just wasn't that kind of guy.

He grabbed life by the horns, he took what he wanted, he lived in the moment, he did whatever felt right to him at the time, and he didn't bother himself with the consequences.

Consequences were for losers.

For people who were too afraid to go for what they wanted because of a list of hypothetical reasons. How could you truly know what would happen when you did something until you actually did it?

He was smart, and he was orderly, he was always thinking ten steps ahead, and he weighed the pros and cons of every single decision that he made, and yet he never let the fact that things could go wrong stop him from forging ahead.

Things hadn't always been this way.

He remembered a time in his life when he had been small and weak, helpless. Back then, he hadn't been in control of his life, but that had all changed one day, a day that was seared into his memory like a brand.

In a way it was a brand.

A brand that marked the change in him as clearly as night and day, black and white, hot and cold.

And that was how different he was.

The before and after.

He had finally decided that he wasn't going to be anyone's punching bag anymore, he was going to take control of his own life.

He shook his head.

He was such a cliché.

Poor little abused boy became angry and violent and took out all the years of helpless fear and pain on innocent bystanders because it was the only way he could make sense of what he had lived through.

With his analytical mind, good looks, fake charm, and the fact that regular emotions and empathy had been beaten out of him, he was basically a monster in human form.

Not that he had actually killed anyone.

Well, not yet anyway.

But he certainly enjoyed inflicting pain so it was only the next logical progression.

A progression he was actually looking forward to.

Not that he was in any hurry, it wasn't like there weren't other fun things he could do that were a lot less risky. Like setting the fire. It wasn't a random fire, he knew what he was doing, and he had a purpose behind it.

A purpose that wasn't achieved yet.

There was more to do and that meant he had to keep busy. Not that he had anything else to do with his life. Thanks to a certain someone, his life had been turned upside down and although he was trying to minimize the fallout, make sure that no one found out, or at least no one realized just how bad things really were because it was pretty hard to hide facts, it didn't mean that he wasn't going to get his revenge.

Since he had a plan he had to keep moving, he couldn't allow himself to worry about the cops, about what they might or might not know about the fire. He couldn't worry about what the people of River's End were thinking or doing, he just had to focus on the plan. He was good at doing that, focusing on the plan at hand had been his mantra ever since that day he had changed, it had served him well, and he was confident that it would continue to serve him well.

Wearing a disguise—tacky and amateurish as it seemed—because it was a practical way to be able to move through the town without anyone paying him any mind, he was out scouting for locations. He had taken quite a liking to starting fires, and he was—quite unexpectantly—looking forward to starting his next one. Now he just had to find the perfect place.

There were so many to choose from, River's End was quite the adorable little town, and while it almost seemed a shame to destroy parts of it, it wasn't such a shame that he wasn't going to do it. He didn't really care about River's End, cute as it was, and he didn't care about the people who lived here, just like he didn't care about the people who lived anywhere else on the planet. He didn't care about people, he just cared about using them as pawns to get what he wanted.

And he had to say he was pretty good at it.

Nodding hello at a passing couple who had their arms wrapped around each other and big smiles on their faces, he fought the urge to roll his eyes.

People were so stupid.

He'd always had a high IQ, and it was so much easier to outsmart people when you were actually smarter than they could even imagine.

He passed an ice cream parlor and the sudden urge to indulge had him diverting into the store. He picked a cone with a scoop of blueberry and a scoop of chocolate, and then because he felt like being decadent for a moment, he decided to sit on one of the wicker chairs outside the parlor and eat before he went back to roaming the town.

This was nice.

It was nice to take a moment just to relax.

His brain was always whirling around at a million miles a second, and while it was useful, it was also exhausting. He didn't take time out just to chill and relax, it felt like such a waste of time, but he would have to remember that occasionally it was important to rest. If he didn't he wouldn't be able to focus properly and he would mess up and make a mistake, and there was no way he was going to do that.

He was going to run this smoothly, perfectly, without any hiccups.

The ice cream break would help him refocus, and then he could work on what came next.

Today would be a rest day, he didn't want to rush because rushing would lead to mistakes as well.

Mistakes.

The bane of his existence.

In all his life he could count the number of mistakes he had made on one hand, those mistakes still haunted him. They made him feel like a failure. Failures didn't flourish only those who were smart, who were careful, who thought about what they were doing did.

He flourished.

He was going to flourish.

He was going to do what he had always done, he was going to work hard, keep his head in the game, and make sure that he walked away with exactly what he wanted.

With a smile, he finished off his ice cream cone then stood and resumed his stroll through the town, confident that his careful planning meant things would go his way.

~

4:56 P.M.

She woke with that all too familiar feeling of the lingering terror a nightmare left you with. Her chest was heaving, her brow sweaty, and she was shivering as though someone had dumped a bucket of ice over her herd.

Maggie would much prefer taking an ice bath than sleeping.

She'd rather *live* in an ice bath than have to go to sleep and face bad dreams.

Soft voices were speaking nearby, and she forced the fear from the nightmare away, coaching herself to calm her ragged breathing and wiping an arm across her forehead to wipe away the beads of sweat that dotted across it.

The movement must have drawn the attention of whoever was whispering because Sheriff Abe Black and Meadow appeared around the corner of the couch.

"Maggie, you're awake. How are you feeling?" Meadow asked, dropping onto the sofa beside her.

"Fine," she lied, but it didn't convince either of them, probably because she winced as the word tore at her aching throat and the cough that accompanied it made it sound like her body was trying to cough up a lung. She hadn't done anything today but lie on the couch, talk with Meadow a little, and sleep, her entire body felt drained and no matter how much she napped it didn't seem to make a difference.

"Drink some water, it'll help," Abe said, handing her a glass of cold water.

The cool liquid felt like heaven flowing down her burning throat, and it not only eased the pain but soothed the coughing as well. "Thanks, that did help," she confessed, her voice sounding like she'd had a lifelong love affair with cigarettes, hopefully that rough rasp would fade soon and her voice could go back to normal.

"Told you," Abe said with a half-smile, and she wondered whether his personal experience with smoke inhalation had come from his time in the military or his time as the sheriff. The Abe she remembered from when she was a kid was vastly different from the man he was today. As a kid, he had been cocky, confident, boisterous, and loud, always had a smile on his face and a joke to crack, but the Abe who had returned from the military was quiet, subdued, rarely smiled, and was typically brisk, although he would move mountains for anyone he cared about. Meadow was softening him up, and when her baby arrived she was sure that little bundle would have the big man wrapped around its tiny finger in a matter of moments.

"Theo stopped by while you were sleeping," Meadow told her, "he dropped off some clothes, and then since I was here, he left again to go run some more errands. You can go and change if you want, and grab something to eat."

She *was* hungry, and wearing something that fit her instead of Theo's oversized clothes would be nice, even if it did mean giving up wearing something that smelled just like him and helped her make believe she was wrapped up in his strong, sturdy arms, but there was something in Abe's face that told her he wasn't just here to check in with his fiancée.

He had news.

Bad news.

And if it was bad news for Meadow he'd tell her at the little cabin they shared.

That meant it was for her.

Since the current source of bad news in her life was the fire, it had to be about that.

"What's wrong?" she asked grimly. She was one of those people who preferred to just rip the Band-Aid right off, so if there was bad news to be given she didn't want to beat around the bush about it, she just wanted him to tell her and get it over with.

"How about Meadow makes something to eat and we have a little dinner first," Abe suggested.

"That bad, huh?"

His bleak face said that it was.

Knowing that bad news was coming only amped up her anxiety. "Just tell me, please, I want to know."

Abe sighed, but he nodded and took a seat on the other sofa. "It's about the fire."

"I assumed it was," Maggie said, not in the mood for his stalling. She had a blinding headache, her whole body felt like it had been filled with lead, and she was still tired enough to sleep for a month, while that feeling of exhaustion wasn't new to her, this bone deep fatigue felt different.

She was tired.

Of her life.

She wanted a break.

She wanted to not feel guilty, even just for a minute.

She wanted there to be a way to right the wrong caused by her past but there wasn't.

"The fire wasn't an accident, it was arson," Abe told her gently, his hazel eyes full of a mixture of compassion and concern.

Arson.

Not an accident like she had assumed.

That meant that someone had *wanted* to burn down her hotel.

Maggie gasped.

Did that also mean that someone had wanted to kill her?

Who?

Why?

This didn't make any sense.

Her head was spinning and obviously it was noticeable because Meadow clucked like a mother hen and wrapped an arm around her shoulder.

"Are you sure?" Maggie asked Abe. Surely there was no way to be one hundred percent positive. Maybe this was all just some big misunderstanding. It had to be, the alternative was something she couldn't comprehend at the moment.

"Positive. Someone doused the place in gasoline before they set it alight," Abe informed her.

So pretending this was a mistake didn't look like a viable option.

Maggie shrunk in on herself, suddenly glad that she was still wearing Theo's t-shirt. It smelled like him, and while it certainly wasn't as good as the real thing it felt like she was wrapped up in his arms. She wasn't sure why he had become her rock all of a sudden, yes they'd been friends for years, but she wasn't any closer to him than she was any of her other friends, but then he'd saved her life, and let her stay with him, and given her mind-blowing orgasms, and now he was the rock in the middle of her shaky life.

"Who started the fire?" she asked.

"I don't know. We're looking through all of the guests who were there and we have a couple of leads," Abe replied vaguely.

"Why would someone set fire to my hotel because of someone who was staying there?" she asked incredulously. This whole thing felt like a dream. Another of her horrible nightmares. She was sure that at any second she would wake, panting and sweaty, and find herself right back in her bedroom in her apartment in the attic of the hotel. None of this would have happened, no fire, no sex with Theo, everything would be just the same as it had always been.

"I don't know yet, Mags, but we'll find who did this, I promise you we will."

She believed him, she really did, but she wasn't sure that getting answers was going to make her feel any better.

Nothing could make this better.

"Maggie," Abe leaned forward, his elbows on his knees, his face earnest, "there's a chance that *you* might have been the target."

Her?

The target?

It wasn't like that hadn't been her first thought—it was her hotel after all—but hearing Abe say it and to know that the cops were looking into it as a viable possibility suddenly made the idea seem very real.

"Is there anyone you can think of who would want to hurt you?" Abe asked.

Of course not.

No one.

Why would anyone want to hurt her?

She kept to herself, she didn't let anyone get too close, she was careful to make sure that no one would figure out her lie, there wasn't anyone who would set fire to her hotel to hurt her or to kill her.

"No," she said softly. Her headache was getting worse and she knew she was trembling even though her body felt detached from her mind because she could see her hands shaking.

"Are you sure?"

"I said no," she said more forcefully this time. "I think I need to go lie down for a while." Standing, she hurried as fast as her weakened body would allow up the stairs.

"Abe and I will stay until Theo gets home," Meadow called out after her.

Upstairs, she hovered in the hall for a moment, unsure which bedroom she should go to. She could—probably should—take one of the spare bedrooms, Theo had made it clear he didn't intend to sleep with her again so getting into his bed seemed wrong, and yet that was where her feet took her. She needed to feel safe and Theo was the only person who had ever made her feel that way.

So good idea or not, she ran into Theo's room and crawled into his bed, snuggling under the covers that smelled just like him.

Then she let her tears fall.

~

5:14 P.M.

Theo put the window up as it started to rain.

After a mostly warm and sunny start to spring it looked like they were finally going to get some spring rains. He liked the rain, in his years in the military, out in the deserts of Afghanistan, the heat and the sand, he'd had enough of it for a lifetime. Rain was soothing to him, the drumming sound of it as it hit the ground, the feel of it cool on his skin, it relaxed him, took him out of his head a little, let him just chill out.

After purchasing and dropping off a few clothes for Maggie, he'd driven out to the hotel, wanting to see the damage for himself. Thankfully, it hadn't been quite as bad as he had been expecting, but he wasn't sure that Maggie would meet her goal of being back open by Fourth of July, but who knows, perhaps if she found a contractor who could start right away and he had a ton of guys he could bring in to work it could happen.

He had to work again tomorrow, starting at eight in the morning, he worked twenty-four-hour shifts, two days off one day on, so he had to figure out what to do with Maggie during the day. It wasn't that she wouldn't be okay on her own, it was just that she'd been through a major trauma, and he didn't like the idea of her sitting around his house lost and alone for hours on end.

Maybe he could call in reinforcements.

His oldest brother Abe's fiancée Meadow worked in the restaurant at the hotel, so she was out of work for as long as it took for the hotel to be rebuilt anyway, maybe she could hang out with Maggie during the day. Maggie would probably see it as having a babysitter, but that wasn't what this was about, he just didn't want her alone and dwelling on everything that had happened.

"Speak of the devil," he said when his phone rang and Meadow's name showed up on the screen.

He pulled over to the side of the road because he never touched his phone while driving, he'd been to too many car wrecks where the driver had been distracted by their cell and crashed, needing him and his crew to cut them from the wreckage. "What's up?" he asked when he answered.

"You need to come back home," Meadow said without preamble.

"Why? Did something happen? Is Maggie okay?" She'd been fine when he'd left, tired, and he knew she was in pain, but he didn't think she'd been in danger of her smoke inhalation getting worse.

"She's okay," Meadow replied quickly. "But Abe came by, he had bad news for her, about the fire, and she's pretty upset."

He muttered a curse under his breath. His brother should have waited until he got back before giving Maggie bad news. Didn't he know how vulnerable she was at the moment? "Put her on," he ordered.

"She ran upstairs," Meadow said on a sigh.

He muttered another curse. "All right, I'll be there in ten." With that he disconnected, tossed the phone back on the passenger seat and took off down the street at close to double the speed limit. He wasn't worried about getting a ticket. His brother was the sheriff, his cousins and his best friend were the deputies, and everyone in River's End loved Maggie, no one would dare even consider giving him a speeding ticket for trying to get to her as quickly as he could.

Despite his ten minute estimate, he was pulling into his driveway in closer to six minutes. Theo grabbed his phone, jumped the three porch steps in one go and flung open his front door.

Abe and Meadow met him in the hall. "It was arson," his brother informed him.

He'd love to say he was surprised, but he'd been a firefighter ever since he left the military and he'd been at the hotel today, he could see from the way the fire had attacked the building that it had been started deliberately.

"You should have waited until I was here before telling her." He sighed.

"I tried to stall but she knew I had bad news," Abe told him.

Of course she had, Maggie was smart and quick as a whip. "I'll go see if she's okay."

He was halfway up the stairs when Meadow called out to him. "She told me about last night."

Theo froze.

That was not good news.

The last thing he wanted was for him and Maggie sleeping together to fly around the local gossip circle.

"Don't tell anyone, please," he said without turning around.

"Don't hurt her," Meadow shot back.

He wanted to say he wouldn't, but truth was he already had by not saying no last night.

Leaving them behind, he took the rest of the stairs by threes and paused as he considered where to look for her. There were three bedrooms including his and he had a sinking feeling that she would have gravitated to his.

When he opened his bedroom door he found her in his bed.

His heart did a strange little pitter-patter, and his stomach dropped, but before he could analyze why he heard the sound of crying.

Maggie was crying.

Damn if that didn't eat right through his soul.

"Hey, sweetheart," he crooned, climbing on top of the covers and drawing her into his arms. She came without protest or resistance and curled into him, her face buried against his neck, her tears wet against his skin.

"Someone did it on purpose," she cried softly. "They deliberately burned down my hotel. Why would someone do that?"

She sounded so sweet, so innocent, so scared, and all he wanted to do was take away her pain. "I don't know, sweetheart, but we'll find out. Abe won't stop until he gets this whole mess sorted out. Shh," he soothed, rubbing circles on her back and wondering what he was going to do to get her to stop crying. He could handle a crying woman, and Maggie had every right to be weeping in his arms right now, she'd just lost her business and her home, and nearly died in the process, and now she knew it hadn't been an accident, but Maggie's tears were different. He cared about her.

"Theo," she said, her voice husky, and he knew she was going to kiss him even before she tilted her face and touched her lips to his jaw.

All his blood suddenly fled to one particular body part, but he gently put his hands on her shoulders and eased her away. "Mags, we can't. We shouldn't. I'm not going to take advantage of you again."

Since Theo knew that she wasn't going to take no for an answer, and he wasn't going to be able to resist her, he quickly stood, gathering her—blankets and all—into his arms.

"What are you doing?" Maggie asked.

"Taking care of you like I should have last night," he informed her. "I'm going to run you a hot bath, then I'm going to go make you comfort food, we'll watch a movie—a chick flick—then I'm going to tuck you into bed so you can get a full night's sleep."

"Chick flick?" Maggie repeated with an amused smile. "You're going to watch a chick flick with me? I thought you said when we were organizing those outdoor movies for the kids last summer that you would rather die than watch chick flicks."

"Yeah, well for you, sweetheart, I'll make an exception this one time," he teased, pleased that she wasn't upset that he'd put a stop to things before they could get out of control like they had last night. He didn't want to hurt Maggie, and leading her on was wrong, she'd latched onto him because he'd been the one to save her, she didn't really want sex with him she just wanted to forget the mess her life had turned into.

"Thank you," she said and kissed his cheek. "You're the best."

"I try." He grinned, relaxing now that he knew that what they'd done last night hadn't ruined their friendship. Setting her down on the bathroom floor, he turned the tap to hot and started running the bath. "Why don't you go grab some of the clothes I bought? I'm sure you'll be glad to get into something that fits, then while you relax in the bath I'll go cook, you can decide what movie you want to watch while you soak."

"You really are the best, Theo," she gushed.

"Ego, baby, remember my ego."

Maggie giggled, and as he left her alone in the bathroom he tried really hard not to think about the fact that she was naked in there. Friend or not, Maggie was sexy as hell and part of him regretted that he'd been the good guy and stopped before they made another mistake.

"You're doing the right thing," he muttered as he stalked downstairs. The right thing, but he was probably going to have to take a cold shower before he went to bed tonight.

April 7th
3:11 A.M.

Flames leaped about her.

Reaching out tendrils, trying to grab her.

Someone walked through the fire.

Theo.

He was coming to save her.

Relief flooded through her, and she dodged the flames running toward him.

But when she got closer she froze.

It wasn't Theo.

It was the face that haunted her nightmares.

"Come to me, Maggie," the face said, his voice sounded like smoke.

"No," she begged. "Please."

"This is what you deserve, you deserve to burn in Hell."

The man started to laugh.

The flames closed in on her.

She was on fire ...

Maggie woke on a strangled scream, her body was burning hot, and she quickly shoved the covers off. As soon as they were off and the cool air touched her sweaty skin she shivered, suddenly ice cold.

Why wouldn't the nightmares leave her alone?

She curled her fingers into fists and pressed them against her closed eyes. She couldn't take much more of this. The nightmares and lack of sleep were killing her. Slowly killing her but killing her just the same. She couldn't go on like this indefinitely, but she didn't know how to break the cycle.

The nightmares had changed over time, but they were always there, they were always hovering over her, even during the day because she knew that she was only hours away from having to go to bed to face them again.

With a resigned sigh, because she knew nothing in her life was ever going to change, Maggie climbed off the bed. She wasn't going to sleep again tonight so she may as well get up. Maybe she'd go downstairs and make herself some hot chocolate, then she'd do a little work on getting things ready to send to the insurance company. No ...

She couldn't do that.

She didn't have her laptop anymore so she couldn't work on her claim.

She didn't have anything anymore.

Maggie stopped herself before she could fall off the edge of the cliff and into a deep sea of self-pity. She was alive and that was something. And as soon as she got a new license and her bank cards back she'd feel more independent again. She had enough money in her accounts to cover her for a while, but because it was arson and not an accident that had started the fire, she wasn't sure how long it would be until the insurance company would pay out.

Things weren't as bad as they could be, and besides, there was nothing she could do about the fire right now so there was no use crying over spilled milk. Everything would get sorted out, Abe would find who had set that fire, the hotel would be rebuilt, it would reopen, she'd move back home, and everything would go back to the way it had been before.

Only she wasn't sure she wanted everything to go exactly back to how it was.

If it wasn't for the fire then she would never have looked at Theo as anything other than her friend.

And she *was* looking at Theo differently.

Last night he had been so sweet, he'd run her a bath, cooked her macaroni and cheese, lasagna, and homemade fries, they'd laughed and talked while they ate, then they'd watched one of her favorite movies, and when she'd fallen asleep snuggled up at his side he must have carried her up to bed and tucked her in.

Could he be any sweeter?

What made it worse—heart-achingly worse—was that while she knew she was developing feelings for him, she knew he wasn't falling for her and was never going to fall for her.

That was just depressing.

Why couldn't everything have stayed the same between them?

Why did she have to ruin everything by telling him she wanted sex?

Why didn't he stop her?

She'd just been through a major traumatic event so he should have been the one to be thinking clearly and stop her from doing something that they could never take back, and that would mean things between them could never be the same.

He'd been right, it was a mistake.

She loved Theo, he was one of her favorite people in the whole world, and now she felt something for him that he would never feel for her. Eventually that would come between them. Her feelings were only going to grow the more time she spent around him, and he would feel uncomfortable, probably like he was leading her on, and there would go the friendship.

"You're an idiot," she muttered to herself as she pulled the blanket off the bed and wrapped it around her before padding out into the hall. It hadn't gone unnoticed that when Theo had brought her upstairs he had put her to bed in one of the spare bedrooms and not in his own bed. If that wasn't a clear enough indication of how he felt about her then nothing was.

As quietly as she could, she tiptoed down the hall and downstairs, she knew that if he heard her up, gentleman that he was, he'd get up too so she wouldn't be alone, and she needed a little alone time.

Given that she was very quickly falling for him he was the last person she wanted to spend time around. This might be a little easier if he didn't have to look so hot all the time. She was a woman, twenty-seven years old, so it wasn't like she never noticed an attractive man, and she had a lot of attractive friends, but they never stirred up these feelings that Theo gave her just by being in the same room as her. He made her stomach feel like it had adopted a carousel and was enjoying riding it a little too much. He made her pulse drum in her ears until it drowned out everything, her self-doubt, her guilt, her desire to punish herself for the bad choices that she had made. He made her heart hammer in her chest, and a weird fluttery feeling fly around inside her, he made her think of sex and that wasn't something she had ever spent much time thinking about.

There was enough light through the curtainless kitchen windows so she didn't turn on a light, anything not to attract Theo's attention, as she set about making hot chocolate. At least he had to go to work today, he'd be leaving after breakfast, and he'd be gone for twenty-four hours, hopefully that would be enough time for her to get a handle on these weird feelings he was making her have.

Because these feelings would fade.

They had to.

She and Theo were friends, and she didn't want that to change, she didn't want to lose him, and he'd saved her life, she was sure that these feelings she was having for him were just because of that and how amazingly sweet he had been following the fire.

That was it.

Nothing more.

The milk began to bubble in the saucepan so she poured it into the mug, then added some chocolate chips and stirred until they melted. Usually she'd melt the chocolate in the microwave first, but she was worried the beeping would wake Theo, so she had to do it this way. Maggie added a couple of marshmallows and then took her drink into the living room and curled up in the comfortable armchair in the corner.

It was quiet which helped her think, she really did believe that these feelings for Theo were just because he had saved her life. He was her knight in shining armor and he'd ridden in on a white horse to save her. She'd be dead if it wasn't for him, of course she thought she was falling in love with him.

Love?

Was it really that bad?

Was she really falling in love with him?

How could things have changed this quickly?

How could she have thought of him as nothing more than a friend just a few days ago and now she was falling in love?

Didn't she have enough to deal with over the fire and losing her home, her business, and everything she owned in one fell swoop? Why was she complicating her life by obsessing over feelings that didn't mean anything more than gratefulness for all that he had done for her?

This would all just pass.

"One problem at a time, Mags," she coached herself. "First let's work on sorting out everything to do with the fire, and by then these feelings or whatever they are will probably be gone anyway."

That sounded legitimate.

She had enough to occupy her mind and once she wasn't just sitting around dwelling on how sweet Theo was then she'd just move on and their friendship could go back to how it had always been.

It sounded so logical and yet ...

Maggie was afraid she really *was* falling in love with Theo.

She was pretty sure there had never been anyone as good at making a mess of their life as she was.

~

6:00 A.M.

He woke in a bad mood.

Bad mood was probably an understatement.

All night Theo had dreamed of Maggie, of the two of them naked in his bed, touching each other, kissing each other, and having hot sex. Waking up alone in his bed meant only one thing.

A cold shower.

That was not how he wanted to start his day.

Shoving the covers off his bed, Theo got out and snatched up his clothes as he headed for the bathroom attached to his bedroom. He'd thought putting Maggie in the spare bedroom would eliminate these feelings and yet they were worse. Theo knew that friends with benefits never worked out, one person always wanted more so someone always got hurt. With him and Amethyst, he'd been the one to get hurt, but between him and Maggie she'd be the one who ended up with a broken heart, and he didn't want to do that to her.

As much as he didn't want to back out on his offer to have her stay with him, if things between them didn't go back to normal, he might have to find her another place to stay.

Turning on the shower, he got in while the water was still cold and let the icy chill dampen some of the sexual need that was flowing through him. He'd thought that things were going back to normal between them last night. Maggie had curled up at his side while they'd watched some movie she liked, and since she'd fallen asleep before it was finished he'd carried her up and put her in the spare bedroom without her having a chance to make another move on him.

They were friends.

He knew sex between friends wasn't a good idea.

So why could his body not get the message?

This was such a bad idea, and Theo knew the best thing for both him and Maggie was for him to send her away. He knew anyone in town would take her, either of his brothers would, or either of his cousins, and staying with Abe, or Will or Julian, would mean she was protected if the arsonist was after her. And yet the thought of her not being here was one he didn't want to consider right now.

Cold showers were going to become his new best friend.

Finishing up in the bathroom, he shrugged into his clothes and walked quietly to the spare bedroom.

Which was empty.

For a moment he panicked. Had something happened to her? Was the fire about her? Had whoever set it found out she was here and come for her? It had been forty-eight hours since the fire so it was unlikely her smoke inhalation had gotten worse, but he wasn't a doctor so what did he know, maybe she'd gotten up in the night and passed out.

Fighting back fear, he took the stairs two at a time and then skidded to a halt in the living room when he saw her curled up in an armchair. She had a blanket tucked around her, her hands were folded together, her pale cheek resting on them, her plump lips forming a small O. Long eyelashes fanned out across her cheeks, and her long chocolate brown locks spilled out over her shoulders.

She looked like a sleeping angel.

Groaning as all the good he'd accomplished with the cold shower was undone, he headed into the kitchen. Maggie was his responsibility while she was staying here and that included feeding her, so he may as well make her breakfast. He knew Maggie loved waffles so he'd whip up a few, he had plenty of time before he had to leave for work. If he was lucky she'd still be asleep when he left and he could enjoy twenty-four hours without having to see her sexy curves, and the way she pouted when she was concentrating, he was sure she didn't know she was doing it, but it made him want to drag her into his arms and kiss her senseless.

Just as he was about to start pouring waffle batter into the waffle maker his phone rang. He should have known better, he always screened his calls, but he was distracted with thoughts of Maggie and her all too kissable lips, and he picked it up and pressed answer before he even really knew what he was doing.

"Theo."

The voice in his ear paralyzed him.

Another arrow shot through his already battered heart.

Since he was a glutton for punishment he didn't just hang up right then and there.

"Amethyst," he said slowly. It didn't matter how many times he reminded himself that she wasn't his and was never going to be, his heart couldn't seem to get that message. It ached just hearing her voice and knowing that all she was ever going to see him as was a friend. A bad friend who hadn't even called her back to congratulate her on her pregnancy. "Hey."

"Don't hey me," Amethyst said sharply. "I called you two days ago to tell you that I'm pregnant and you never got back to me."

He could be honest and tell her that the thought of her pregnant with another man's baby made him feel ill, or he could lie.

Lie it was.

"Yeah, sorry, Am, things kind of got crazy around here. A friend of mine her hotel burned down, I only just got her out in time. She's a mess, and she needs someone right now, and that someone is me, she's staying with me, and I've kind of been preoccupied with taking care of her. I got your message though, congratulations." He forced the word through his throat that threatened to close up on him.

"Thanks, and okay," Amethyst said sullenly. "I get why you didn't call me back. Is your friend okay?"

"Smoke inhalation, and she's upset losing her home and her business, and then she got another blow when she found out the fire was deliberately set." At least he wasn't lying in anything he'd told her, he was just neglecting to mention that Maggie wasn't the reason he hadn't called back, it was that he was selfish enough to wish it was his baby she was carrying instead of her husband's.

"I'm so sorry to hear that, but at least she's alive, and it sounds like she has you to thank for that, I'm sure she thinks of you as her hero."

Maggie did.

That was part of the problem.

He'd saved her life and that had changed everything between them.

"Yeah, I guess. Look, Am, I have to go, I'm cooking breakfast, and I have to be at work in an hour. I'll talk to you later, okay?"

"Yeah okay, call if there's anything we can do to help your friend."

And there it was.

The reason he loved Amethyst.

She didn't even know Maggie, she lived four hours away, she was recently married and expecting her first child, she had three sisters who were also married with young children, and she and her family had suffered more than their fair share of trauma and heartache, and yet she was offering to help someone else in need.

Could the woman be any more perfect?

"Thanks, Am. Bye," he said and quickly hung up.

There had to be something wrong with him. He was hopelessly in love with a woman who had never seen him as anything but a friend. He was missing out. Theo knew that. There were a lot of great women out there, women who would actually love him back, and yet he was so hung up on Amethyst he couldn't let it go.

"You cooking again?"

Theo turned to find Maggie standing in the kitchen doorway. She had a smile on her face, her long hair hung in waves down her back, she was wearing only baggy PJ pants and an oversized sweatshirt and yet she looked sexy enough that he reconsidered his no more sex plan and very nearly took her on the table.

"Yeah, cooking breakfast," he said tightly, turning away because it was the only way he could resist ripping her clothes off.

"What are you making?"

"Waffles."

"I love waffles," she said delightedly. "You know you're going to make me fat if you keep cooking for me every day until my hotel is fixed."

"I guess," he muttered, when what he really wanted to say was that Maggie was stunning, gorgeous, beautiful inside and out, and that it was his pleasure to take care of her in her time of need.

Why couldn't he just say that?

Because Amethyst was still the woman of his dreams.

Because he was worried about leading Maggie on.

Because he was a coward.

Picking up on his grouchy attitude, Maggie didn't say anything else, just took a seat at the table.

Theo cursed his bad mood. He was usually the antithesis of grumpy, he'd seen a lot in his time in the military and as a firefighter, but he'd always managed to hold onto his sense of humor and his easygoing nature. So what was wrong with him now?

What was it about the pretty brunette sitting at his table that made him want to simultaneously strip her naked and have passionate sex with her, bundle her up in his arms and take away all that she was going through, and hold her at arm's length and not let her get any closer to him?

~

12:24 P.M.

"This would look great on you, it's totally your color." Meadow held up a fluffy pink sweater.

Maggie took it and immediately ran the soft material over her cheek. Her friend was right, the pale pink was her favorite color, and the darker pink heart over where your heart would be when you were wearing it was a nice addition.

"They also have it in lavender, cornflower, and mint green," Meadow told her because her friend knew that she often bought multiples of something she liked if it was offered in different colors.

"No yellow?" she asked. Pink was her favorite color and at least three-quarters of the clothes she'd had in her wardrobe had been pink, but her second favorite color was yellow, her favorite shade was daffodil, and she would have loved this sweater in that.

"None that I can see," Meadow replied, searching through the line of sweaters just to make sure.

"Oh well, I do love it in the pink, and it's pretty in the other colors as well, I'll take all four." She grabbed one of each color of the heart sweaters in her size and popped them into the basket. Yesterday Theo had picked up a couple of basics, some jeans and sweatshirts, but she needed underwear, and PJs, dresses, skirts, shirts, t-shirts, she needed a whole new wardrobe, and since it wasn't like her clothes were coming back she'd thought she may as well just come and do it now, then at least she'd feel like she wasn't just floating along in the world with nothing to hold on to.

Maggie was ready to start getting her life back.

Starting with this shopping trip.

Meadow had turned up not long after Theo had left to go to the station, and she had a sneaking suspicion that her friends had been talking about her behind her back and decided that she shouldn't be left alone. Not that she was complaining, she liked Meadow and they always had a good time together, so once they finished shopping for a whole new wardrobe they'd do lunch, and then maybe she'd ask Meadow if she and Abe would like to stay for dinner.

Theo would be at work until tomorrow so she'd be alone in his house, and as much as being alone was her normal, for some reason she didn't want to face the night by herself.

For once—just once—it would be so nice to have someone by her side.

Asking Meadow to spend all day with her was selfish. Her friend was not only seven months pregnant but had spent two weeks in the hospital just two months ago, and while she'd slowly gotten her strength back, Maggie knew that she still got tired easily and was hanging out for her pregnancy to be over and her baby to be born.

She'd be fine on her own.

She was always fine on her own.

"You need anything else in here?" Meadow asked.

"No, I think I have everything I need." The sweaters joined another six sweaters, five blouses, two coats, eight t-shirts, six cardigans, seven skirts, nine dresses, and four pairs of pants. She'd probably continue to pick up a few more things over the next couple of weeks, but she had enough to keep her going.

"Once we finish up here we can go buy you some underwear," Meadow said as they made their way over to the cashier.

Maggie caught the underlying meaning that her friend was hinting about but wasn't going to come right out and say, and it certainly wasn't a conversation she wanted to have. What was there to say anyway? That she had probably ruined her friendship with Theo beyond repair because she'd badgered him into having sex with her, something he hadn't been shy about telling her he regretted and thought was a big mistake. She wasn't so stupid that she was going to throw herself at him again, but it didn't seem to matter, he'd been angry with her this morning, and she suspected that despite their nice evening last night the damage was already done.

Thankfully, Meadow didn't push and they made their purchases and then headed out into the overcast morning. She missed the sunshine, she wanted a ray of brightness in her life even if it was just from the sun, and couldn't really penetrate into her life and brighten it up.

"So ..." Meadow looked at her expectantly.

"So, what?" she asked, not sure what her friend was expecting her to say.

"So, what is going on with you and Theo?"

"Nothing," she answered simply. A horrible thought occurred to her. "You haven't told anyone, have you?"

"Of course not." Meadow looked offended by the notion, but then her cheeks turned pink. "Well, I did tell Abe. But I tell him everything, and you know he's not a gossip, he won't say anything to anyone."

Both Abe and Meadow were about the last people in town to gossip, so she was confident that no one else would find out. The last thing she wanted right now was for any other guys in town to think that the fire had messed with her head and she was now willing to put out for any one of them. She'd been asked out a lot but she always turned men down, and she didn't want anyone to think that that had changed.

"So ..." Meadow prompted again.

"So, what?" she repeated. "I already told you that there is nothing going on between Theo and me. He thinks it was a mistake, and he's going to great lengths to make sure it doesn't happen again. I wouldn't be surprised if within a day or two he suggests that I go and stay with someone else until my hotel is fixed." That hurt in a weird kind of way that it probably shouldn't. While Theo was wishing he could take back what they'd done, here she was wishing that there was more to it.

"Theo might think it was a mistake, but you don't." Meadow was studying her from probing blue eyes. "You want something more."

Maggie shrugged helplessly. It was too hard to describe the swirling mixture of emotions inside her. Part of her *did* want there to be more than just friendship between her and Theo, just because she had never seen him as anything more than a friend before didn't change the fact that for her things had changed when they'd slept together. Part of her was terrified of those feelings, she didn't date, she didn't daydream about a future with a husband and kids, she kept to herself because she believed she deserved to be punished. And part of her was hurt that it had meant so little to Theo. Okay, so he didn't have to be developing feelings for her like she was for him, but he could at least have enjoyed it and not told her it was a mistake.

"You should be honest with him," Meadow told her.

"What tell him that I can't stop thinking about what we did and that I want more but won't actually take more? He'll think I'm crazy." Or worse, he'd want to know why she wanted more but wouldn't take it. "He's made his position clear, he just wants to be friends. He wants to pretend that we never slept together, to him it was a mistake, he wanted sex with Amethyst Hatcher and instead he got me."

"You say that like you're not good enough for him. Well, you know what? I think that that stupid soon to be brother-in-law of mine isn't good enough for you. So maybe Theo isn't the one for you, but maybe he's helped you finally reach a place in your life where you can let go of the guilt and have the future you deserve. Mags, I don't know exactly what you lived through as a child, but I know what it's like to live with someone who hurts you, who tells you that you're not good enough, that makes you feel unworthy, but you have to know that's not true. You're wonderful, and sweet, and beautiful, and you deserve all the happiness in the world. Maybe you don't quite believe it yet, but maybe these feelings you have for Theo are a sign, a sign that you're almost there, almost to that point where you can start planning a real future that involves more than just your hotel."

That was the difference between her and Meadow.

They'd both been beaten down, but while she had retreated inside herself, satisfied to spend her life hiding, Meadow had become more determined to find the happiness she craved.

What Maggie wouldn't give to have even a tiny piece of Meadow's determination ...

Her train of thought was shattered when something suddenly exploded, and she and Meadow were thrown through the air.

She landed on the pavement with a thump that shuddered painfully through her body, then fire sprung up around her.

~

12:43 P.M.

. . .

"That makes ten points for me, one more and I win." Theo grinned at Keith.

"I could still make a comeback," Keith growled.

Theo just laughed. Keith hadn't beaten him in ping pong in the six months since he had transferred to work as part of the River's End fire department. The department actually covered River's End and five other nearby small towns and the freeways and highways that connected them.

He missed his old team, but he already loved his new one. Although Keith hadn't grown up in River's End and they'd only known each other for a few months, they were already great friends. When they were at the firehouse waiting for a callout they passed the time playing ping pong, darts, pool, poker, and when they got bored of trying to beat each other they might take a break and read or watch TV.

Keith was happily engaged to a gorgeous, bubbly, smart young woman who taught second grade at the local school, and he couldn't deny that he was jealous. That could be him. If Amethyst had never fallen for Zeb Tuck then it could be him who'd won her heart, who'd made her his wife, who'd impregnated her.

But it wasn't.

And he had to find a way to get over it.

The sooner the better because he didn't like this bad-tempered, mopey, wallowing in self-pity version of himself.

It was time.

Time to let go of the past and the could have beens.

He was done.

Theo straightened his spine, he was ready. He was ready to leave the past where it belonged and accept reality for what it was, and the first thing he had to do was apologize to Maggie for being grumpy with her this morning.

"Give it up and just accept that I'm always going to beat you ..." Theo trailed off as the siren sounded.

"Tie game." Keith grinned as he tossed his paddle onto the table.

"You got lucky, but you know I still would have won," he shot back as he dropped his paddle as well.

A minute later, he and Keith and the rest of their team were climbing into the fire truck, lights flashing and sirens screaming, as they headed off toward whoever was in need of their services. He prayed it was going to be an easier call out than the last one had been. Not that any callout was easy, whether they were using the jaws of life to pull someone out of a wrecked vehicle, or putting out a fire in someone's home or business, lives were irrevocably changed.

It was what had led him into this job in the first place.

Fresh out of the military, struggling to adapt to life as a civilian, he had known that law enforcement wasn't the route he wanted to go, it was something about dealing with victims of crime that left him uneasy and way out of his depth, so the fire department had seemed like a good choice. He still got to help people, but he didn't have to deal with victims past getting them out of a burning building or crashed vehicle.

They didn't drive for long, less than five minutes later they were turning into Main Street, and he could see the flames dancing about. It looked like a car was on fire, it was parked at the side of the road, and pieces of burning debris were dotted about in the ten feet or so encircling the vehicle.

"What happened?" he asked. Since the car was sitting there parked and there were no others around it, it hadn't been involved in an accident. The hairs on the back of his neck stood up, something was wrong. Since he knew that the fire at Maggie's hotel had been deliberately set, he wondered if this was another case of arson.

"Car exploded," Dirk replied.

Explosion.

That was suspicious if ever he'd heard it.

They pulled to a stop, and it wasn't until they'd all gotten out and were shooting water at the flaming car that he saw her.

Maggie.

She was sitting huddled against the wall of a shop not fifteen feet from where the explosion had occurred. She was alone, and even from here he could see the haunted look on her face and the small red marks on her paper pale skin.

She'd been here.

Two fires in less than a week and she'd been present for both of them.

"You got this?" he asked his team, he had to go to her. Why was she alone? Why wasn't someone taking care of her?

"Yeah, go check on her, we'll have this out in no time, it's already dying down," Dirk told him.

Nodding a quick thanks at his lieutenant, Theo hurried over to Maggie, crouching at her side and noting the delay it took her to register his presence.

"Theo?" she asked, her voice quiet and shaky.

"Yeah, sweetheart, it's me. What happened?" He reached for her hands, found them freezing, and began to rub them between his briskly.

"Fire," she murmured, her gaze returning to the blaze, which was dwindling by the second.

"Were you here when it exploded?" he asked. It was clear from the dozens of tiny cuts he could see on her face and hands—no doubt from the shattering glass—that she had been, but he wanted to get her talking.

Maggie nodded slowly as though it were suddenly very heavy.

She was clearly in shock, and although her injuries appeared minor, she still needed medical attention. There could be glass or other debris lodged in her wounds. "Why hasn't someone checked you out?" he asked, not really expecting her to answer. There were medics about, he could see the ambulance, so why hadn't one of them looked at Maggie?

"Meadow was with me, they wanted to check me out but I told them to look at her first, she's pregnant." Her watery brown eyes met his. "The flames ... they ... I ... it's ... I guess I'm a little wary of fire since, well, you know." Her gaze dropped down, and a little color tinted her cheeks as though she felt this was a shortcoming. Anyone who had nearly died in a fire just a few days ago would be at the very least uneasy being around flames again so soon.

Theo gently grasped her chin and tilted her face up. "There's nothing wrong with that, Mags. I am a little worried about you though, you're pale, a little disoriented, you have at least a dozen cuts that I can see, and your pulse is racing."

She dragged in a breath, and he could see she was internally lecturing herself to pull it together. Part of him hated that she felt like she had to put on a front when she was with him, they were friends, they'd slept together, she was living in his house, there was no need for her to pretend with him.

"I'm okay," she told him. "A little shaken up, but I'm okay. You don't need to stay with me."

While she'd said the words, her fingers had curled around his, gripping on tightly, saying the words her mouth couldn't. "It's okay, Mags," he said, giving her a tender smile. "I'm all yours for the moment. My team is fine, they can handle this, the fire is almost out anyway, and I can catch them up at the firehouse later."

"You're not supposed to go off on your own while you're on shift," she reminded him.

"Stop worrying," he soothed. "The guys can hang out here for a bit while I make sure you're okay, then I'll make sure someone is going to take you home and stay with you."

"I really am fine, Theo. There's absolutely no need for you to be concerned." Her gaze met his squarely, and there wasn't a hint of a tremble in her voice, but it was that very carefully schooled in control façade that told him that she was the opposite of fine.

This woman was always so determined that no one should ever get an inkling that she was anything but calm, cool, and collected, but he saw through the charade. Maggie had a vulnerability to her that she tried to hide, a fragility that had nothing to do with lack of inner strength, that was as obvious to him as her bright eyes and silky hair.

"How about we let someone with medical training determine if you're fine or not," he told her. Then without giving her a chance to argue, he scooped her off the ground and into his arms as he went in search of the medics. Once he knew that she was in fact okay, he'd find someone to cover the rest of his shift because it suddenly seemed like the most important thing in the world that he was with her right now.

She needed him, and he had to be there for her.

It was as simple as that.

Or perhaps it was the most complicated situation he had ever found himself in.

~

3:54 P.M.

She was nervous.

Edgy.

Couldn't sit still or settle to anything.

Maggie was moving restlessly around Theo's house. She'd sit for a bit then get up and go to the bathroom even though she didn't really need to use it, she'd drift to the kitchen, but she wasn't really hungry, then back to the living room again, where she'd try to sit and watch TV, but her mind was buzzing at a million miles a minute and as a result her body had to join it.

She knew she was bothering Levi, and she was trying to sit still, she really was, but she just couldn't.

Theo had stayed with her while some paramedics had checked out the dozens of small cuts she'd gotten when the explosion destroyed the car she and Meadow had been walking past. As she'd told him, they were all minor, and after cleaning them and putting some antibiotic cream on them they'd told her she was free to go.

Only she hadn't really been free to go.

Next up had been the cops, and she'd given her statement and answered what felt like hundreds of questions. Going over and over things had made her head spin, and it hadn't stopped yet.

She had expected—hoped—that Theo would stay with her, bring her back here, hang out with her, help her take her mind off everything that was going on, but he hadn't. He must have called his brother in because Levi had shown up and taken Theo's place beside her while their cousin Will peppered her with questions. Theo had apologized for having to leave and promised he'd be home as soon as he could, but she knew that he worked twenty-four-hour shifts so she wouldn't see him again until tomorrow.

That seemed like an eternity.

Seeing those flames dancing around her had thrown her right back to her hotel when she'd found fire consuming it. She'd felt paralyzed, her lungs had frozen, she couldn't get enough oxygen, the world had started to go gray around the edges, and if Meadow hadn't grabbed her arm and dragged her away from the burning debris then she probably would have ended up with much more serious injuries.

Now she couldn't get the fire out of her head.

She would be thrilled if she never had to see a flame again for the rest of her life. Even the idea of the tiny little flickering flame on a birthday candle sent shivers rippling through her.

"Mags, could you please try to stay still for more than a minute at a time?" Levi asked when she stood up again.

"I am trying."

He switched off the TV then turned to face her. "You want to talk?"

"Not really," she said but dropped back down into her chair. She liked Levi, he looked a lot like Theo with his dark hair, hazel eyes, and chiseled physique, and she'd known him just as long as she had Theo, but she'd never been as close with him as she was with his younger brother. Maybe because Theo was closer in age to her, but whatever the reason, it was Theo she wanted here right now not Levi.

Theo made her feel safe.

He'd walked through flames for her, he'd opened up his home to her, he'd slept with her because it was what she needed at that moment even though he had thought it was a bad idea. He was her rock, and right now when the world seemed like a terrifying place that could throw her into the depths of Hell in a second, she needed a rock.

"Maggie, I know these last few days have been rough on you. Maybe you should consider finding someone who you are comfortable talking to. You don't want to let this all build up inside you. You need to get it out, if you want I can give you some names of some post-traumatic stress counselors."

Maggie appreciated the offer.

She truly did.

And yet there was no way she was taking him up on it. She was an expert in dealing with things herself and burying them deep down inside her soul where there wasn't a chance that they might slip out and get loose.

She was about to open her mouth to decline as politely as she could when the front door swung open and a huge grin spread over her face. "Theo."

"Hey, Mags." He grinned back at her.

"You here to stay?" Levi asked.

"Yep, I was able to find someone to cover the rest of my shift, so just like I promised I'm all yours for the rest of the day. Thanks for hanging here, Levi," Theo said, giving his brother a dismissive smile.

"Sure, happy to help." Levi gave them both a funny look then waved a hand and disappeared out the door, leaving her alone with Theo.

Immediately it was like all the blood in her body pooled between her legs, every nerve ending seemed to lead there, making her suddenly uncomfortable and very needy. She wanted his hands on her body, his lips crushed against hers, she wanted him buried deep inside her, she wanted to come on a rush of indescribable bliss screaming his name. But it wasn't like she could beg Theo for sex. He'd made it perfectly clear that he wasn't interested in doing that again, so she was going to have to get that idea out of her head.

Theo came and sat beside her, reaching for her hands, and from the look on his face she knew he had something he needed to tell her. "Maggie, about this morning, I wasn't in the best of moods and I took it out on you."

"It's fine." She brushed it off like it was no big deal.

"No, it's not, there's no excuse for being rude, and I'm sorry."

She smiled, he had hurt her feelings but he sounded sincere, and it wasn't like she'd never been in a bad mood before and taken it out on someone else. "Apology accepted."

"You're something else, you know that?" he asked as he brushed his knuckles across her cheek.

Her eyes zeroed in on his lips. She knew what it felt like to kiss him, and right now, her own lips were practically crying out for him. Maggie shook her head to clear it. "So, uh, I didn't mean to eavesdrop this morning, but it was Amethyst on the phone. Any chance things are going to work out between you two?" She tried not to hold her breath as she awaited his answer, they were only friends, it wasn't like she had any claim on him whether he was with Amethyst or not, and yet she wanted to know if he really could get the woman out of his system.

"Nope, Amethyst is married and they're expecting their first baby. Hard as it is to accept Amethyst was never as into me as I was into her, it is what it is. Maggie, that's why I said we shouldn't sleep together again. I know that you've been through Hell these last few days and I know you needed a distraction, and while that wasn't the best one, I'm glad I was there for you, but I don't want sex to ruin our friendship like it ruined my friendship with Amethyst."

How could she be mad about it when he phrased it like that?

And she wasn't angry with him anyway, she wanted more than he could give her, and she felt like she shouldn't want it anyway. Why should someone like her end up with a wonderful man, and children of her own, and a picture-perfect life?

"Would you take it back if you could?" she asked softly.

"Take what back?"

"Sex, with Amethyst."

"Yes," he said simply. "If I could take it back and just go back to thinking she was a drop-dead gorgeous friend then I would in a heartbeat.

Would you take back sex with me?

That was what she wanted to know, but she was too afraid of the answer to ask the question.

So she kept her mouth shut.

Sometimes it was better to live in blissful ignorance than to have your heart shattered into a million pieces, and Maggie thought that if he told her he wished he could take back what they'd shared it would crush her. She was a little more vulnerable at the moment than she cared to admit, even to herself.

"So I have the perfect way to spend the rest of the day," Theo said, the intensity draining away, her light-hearted friend in his place.

"Oh, yeah?"

"Mario Kart 8 Deluxe."

"You want to play video games?" Maggie didn't spend much time playing video games, she was too busy running a hotel, and she suspected that that was part of the reason he wanted to play, Theo loved to win, and he knew he was going to beat the pants off her.

Well, he thought he was anyway.

But she was a quick learner, and she had played several musical instruments as a child so she had great fine motor skills. She was pretty sure that Theo would beat her the first few times, but then she'd give him a run for his money.

"You want to make this interesting?" she asked.

"You want to place bets?" Theo asked with a wide smile, no doubt thinking about how he was going to spend her money.

"Yep, and don't you go thinking it's going to be like taking candy from a baby," she warned.

"Of course not," he snickered. "You go grab snacks, and I'll get things set up."

All thoughts of the fire gone, replaced instead by dreams of what a future with Theo could be like, Maggie hurried into the kitchen to grab whatever snacks she could find in the cupboards. She didn't know how much time she had to enjoy moments like this so she had to make the most of them.

April 8th
2:07 A.M.

Sleep obviously wasn't happening tonight.

Theo had laid in bed for hours, tossing and turning, trying to shut his brain down enough for it to drift off, but all he could think about was Maggie. Her smile of triumph when she finally beat him in Mario Kart, her laugh as he teased her, the way her thigh felt pressed up against his as they sat side by side on the couch racing each other on track after track.

When at last she had yawned, her sleepy eyes heavy, he'd told her they should call it quits and promised they would play again tomorrow. Then before he could even decide whether to give in to temptation and kiss her she had stood, wished him sweet dreams, and headed up the stairs.

He knew she hadn't done it on purpose, but the way her backside looked as she took each step—a little slowly because he knew she was stiff and sore after being knocked down in the explosion—almost had him running up after her. It would be so easy, snatch her up into his arms, take her to his room, throw her down on the bed, rip off her clothes, then ravish every inch of her body with his hands and his tongue, then sink deep inside her and come with her name falling from his lips.

But he hadn't done that.

Instead, he'd tidied up downstairs, making sure he gave her plenty of time to tuck her pretty little backside into bed before he ventured up. The light had been off in the spare bedroom so he'd been able to make it to his room without any more temptation. Thoughts of Maggie continued to plague him, and realizing that he wasn't going to get much sleep tonight he decided he might as well get up.

Maybe he'd play a little more Mario Kart, Maggie had gotten good quickly, and what he'd thought was going to be easy money had ended up being quite the challenge. He was sure that by the end of the week she'd be able to beat him with her eyes closed and he'd be broke.

"Oh," he said, surprised when he reached the bottom of the stairs and found Maggie curled up in the same armchair she'd been sleeping in when he'd gotten up yesterday morning.

"Sorry, I thought you were asleep." Maggie bounded up so quickly she sent the blanket that had been wrapped around her shoulders falling to the floor. She was wearing just a pair of short shorts and a tank top, and he stared at her long, lean legs as he imagined them wrapped around his waist as he thrust into her. Maggie cleared her throat. "Uh, I'll go back upstairs if you wanted some time to yourself."

She was halfway across the room when he snapped to his sense. "No, stay. Please."

Maggie stopped, but she still appeared uncertain. "I didn't think you'd be up."

"You don't sleep much do you?" he asked. As kids they'd both attended sleepovers together, and there had even been a couple of parties at various friends' houses around town where some of them had spent the night, and now that he thought about it she had always been up before everyone else.

"Bad dreams," she said with a shrug like it was no big deal, but she was tired, and she wasn't able to hide the haunted look in her eyes quickly enough.

No stranger to bad dreams, they'd plagued him a lot in those first few months after he'd left the military, he smiled sympathetically. "They're the worst."

"Mmhmm." She nodded but looked eager to move onto another topic of conversation. "You want to play more Mario Kart?"

"Nope."

"Oh, then what do you want to do? Do you want me to go back upstairs? Do you want something to eat? Do you want to watch TV? We can watch your choice of movie if you want, or we can—"

Theo cut her off by sweeping an arm around her waist and yanking her hard up against him, then crushing his mouth to hers, kissing her like he'd wanted to do ever since the night they spent together. He knew what he wanted to do, and from the way Maggie had been casting surreptitious glances at his bare chest he knew what she wanted to spend the night doing.

The exact same thing he did.

They'd already had sex once, and as tonight had proved it hadn't managed to come between them and ruin their friendship.

So why not?

They were friends, he knew Maggie was still shaken about the fire and the explosion, if she needed something to take her mind off it all, even just for a little while, then shouldn't he, as her friend, give her that?

"Wh-what are you doing?" she stuttered when he ended the kiss.

"Kissing you," he said as he let his fingers trail down her soft cheek.

"Why?" Her chestnut eyes looked up at him, searching his face, trying to seek the answers that she needed.

"Because you want this, maybe even need it, and I'm your friend. If I can't do this for you then I'm not a very good friend am I?"

Maggie opened her mouth, but he cut off whatever she was going to say by kissing her again as he scooped her up into his arms. Carrying her up the stairs, he went to the spare bedroom instead of his room, hoping that might keep a bit of distance between them. As much as he wanted to give Maggie what she needed, he didn't want to lead her on. They were friends, and this was nothing more than one friend helping out another, he didn't want to muddy the waters by implying an intimacy that they could never have.

Laying her gently down on the bed, he took a moment to look at her. Long, dainty limbs, milky white skin, long brown waves cascading over the pillow, those big eyes looking up at him anxiously. He didn't want her anxious, he wanted her so far gone that all she thought about was how he was making her feel and everything that had happened in the last few days faded into nothingness.

Stretching out beside her, he trailed a line of kisses down her slender neck, nibbling on her shoulder. "You wearing anything under the shorts?" he asked as his hand slipped under the waistband to find her bare. "You aren't," he said with a wicked grin. He touched her and she moaned her pleasure. "Bare and ready." Whether this was a good idea or not it certainly stroked his ego to know that Maggie was wet just thinking about him touching her.

While his fingers teased her, he pushed up the hem of her tank top, exposing the most beautiful pair of breasts he had ever seen. When his lips closed over her nipple she sighed, a breathy little sound that almost made him lose control and ditch foreplay to bury himself inside her.

His tongue swirled her nipple, and she arched off the bed, silently begging for more. "You keep making those soft little moans and this is going to be over pretty quickly," he warned.

Her eyes—hooded with desire—looked up at him. "You're so good."

Now it was his turn to groan. "Maybe we go hot and heavy this round, and then I'm going to make you beg before I let you come again."

Her cheeks heated but her body moved restlessly when he withdrew his fingers. Theo shoved his sweatpants off and slipped on a condom, then he thrust into her in one smooth move.

She gasped as he filled her up, then her legs moved to wrap around his waist—just as he had imagined them doing just minutes before—drawing him deeper inside her.

This wasn't going to take long. He was so close he had to force himself to hold back because he knew that Maggie wasn't there yet. He began to move, slow at first, then faster, he could see by the way she met him thrust for thrust that she was getting closer. Closer but not quite there. He wasn't going to be able to hold on much longer, kissing those sweet, plump lips, he reached between them, touching her as he thrust harder and deeper, and a moment later she clamped around him as she came, his name falling from her lips.

He came a second later, groaning Maggie's name as the strongest orgasm of his life flowed through him. It seemed to go on forever, wave after wave of pleasure until he was spent and sagged down on the bed, careful to prop himself on his elbows so his weight didn't crush Maggie.

"Told you, you were good." Maggie's twinkling eyes were the first thing he saw when his vision returned.

No, *he* wasn't good, *they* were good.

Together.

And it wasn't just the mind-blowing sex, he and Maggie had fun together, they hung out together, made each other laugh, and the more time he spent around her the more she was relaxing, letting him in a little.

This was exactly why the whole friends with benefits thing didn't work.

Feelings started creeping in and then before you knew it, the friendship was over.

Tonight he wasn't going to worry about that.

Tonight he was just going to give Maggie what she wanted.

Tonight he had vowed to make Maggie come over and over again until she was exhausted enough to sleep.

"I seem to remember you liked a few of my other moves." He winked at her as he tossed the condom into the wastebasket and moved down the bed. When his tongue touched her, and she sucked in a breath, her fingers curling into the bedsheets, all his doubts fled away. He and Maggie would be okay, and seeing the look on Maggie's face at this moment was worth the risk.

~

9:19 A.M.

. . .

This case had taken a detour and had now hit way too close to home.

Abe stared angrily at the file in front of him, no one messed with his fiancée.

No one.

Especially not some kid who liked causing trouble and starting fires.

Lucky for the Hattock kid, Meadow hadn't been badly injured in the explosion, a couple of cuts and bruises from being thrown to the ground. If she'd been hurt worse than that, then he would have had the kid's head on a platter. Since Meadow was seven months pregnant, he insisted that she take a trip to the hospital to have an ultrasound done to make sure that there were no issues with the baby.

That second when he'd gotten the call to say that Meadow had been in an explosion and before he was told that she was okay had seemed like a lifetime. A lifetime filled with nothing but terror.

It wasn't until he'd seen her with his own eyes, held her in his arms, felt her heart beat against him, and her warm breath against his skin, that he had in fact believed that she was all right. The relief he'd felt had almost knocked him to his knees. He loved that woman completely. She was a part of him, even when she wasn't with him she was, inside his heart, inside his soul, she was a part of him now and he could no more lose her than his leg and still be a whole person.

He loved that baby growing inside her as well.

It didn't matter that he wasn't the biological father, that was *his* child she was carrying. They had decided to wait until the baby was born to find out the gender and he was torn between wanting a son or a daughter. There were pros and cons to each, and a major con to having a little girl was that she might end up with someone like the kid who he was sure had set the fire at Maggie's hotel and the explosion that could have stolen his soon to be wife and child from him.

"I want this kid brought in for questioning," he growled at his cousin.

"We don't have enough for a warrant," Julian reminded him.

"Then we'll interview him as a witness," he snapped. While he knew Meadow wasn't the target of the kid's pyromaniac games, he would still feel safer once the kid was locked away.

"We can probably do that given he was at the hotel and he was there yesterday when the explosion occurred, but only if the foster parents agree to bring him in."

"We'll get a court order if they refuse, the kid is a material witness in two cases. What do we have on the parents?" Since the fire they had been splitting their time looking into everyone on their suspect list from the guests at Maggie's hotel, but after yesterday, when the kid and his foster family had been in the street when the explosion went off they had focused on them. Specifically the kid, Mike Voight. He'd gone to the hospital with Meadow, then taken her home. As much as he loved his job she would *always* come first, so his deputies had started digging into Mike and the Hattock family more closely.

"Ben and Veronica Hattock, forty-six and forty-three respectively, married for twenty-two years. Both work as teachers, him as a high school math teacher and her as an elementary school art teacher. Neither have a record, he has a couple of speeding tickets, she has a few parking tickets, seems like she gets distracted, loses track of time when she's shopping, but nothing nefarious. Their first child was born about five years after they married, he died three years later."

"Cause of death?"

"Fall down the stairs."

Abe arched a brow at that. That wasn't a typical cause of death for a three-year-old child. "History of abuse?"

"Nothing that's recorded, but the child didn't attend daycare or preschool, no nanny or babysitters, limited contact with family. Veronica left her job when she fell pregnant, said she wanted to be a stay at home mom, so the little boy wasn't seen very often."

"You said first child. They had another?" Abe asked.

"A girl, three years after the son's death."

"She died as well?"

"When she was four, a camping accident, she fell over a cliff."

"So two children, both died as preschoolers, both died in falls, I'm guessing the girl didn't have any more contact with the outside world than her brother did?" When Julian nodded, he continued, "So for all we know both children were being abused and were murdered."

"No proof of abuse, but no proof there wasn't," Julian agreed.

"So, we could be looking at abuse on the foster kids as well." To be honest, Abe was surprised that they had been accepted as foster parents with two deceased children, both of who died in suspicious circumstances. But if both deaths had been ruled accidental, then there was no reason for the system, which was desperate for families to take on the thousands of children who needed a home, to not have accepted them.

"That's a definite possibility."

"How long have the kids been with them, and have there been others?"

"They've been foster parents for six years now," Julian replied. "Besides the two current kids there have been another three. Seems like they requested to take in teenagers, the three they had were with them from late teens until they aged out."

That was interesting. Teenagers were a lot harder to control than small children if indeed one or both of the Hattocks were abusive. "And any of those three make complaints against their foster parents?"

"Nothing on record."

"What about Mike or Bessie?"

"Again, nothing on record."

"So as far we know—or can prove—the Hattocks are just a couple with really bad luck who tragically lost two children and now take in foster kids, teenagers at that." Most people who fostered preferred to take in babies or young children, usually teenagers who hadn't already been placed somewhere either aged out of a group home, or were bounced about from house to house, but Mike and Bessie had been with the Hattocks for three years now.

"Teenagers with psychological issues," Julian added. "The previous three kids they had were all kids with behavioral problems, they'd been expelled or suspended, had trouble making friends, petty theft or assault charges, drugs and alcohol issues."

"So they're either trying to make a difference in the world, helping kids in need because they couldn't save their own, or they're deliberately targeting kids who are vulnerable and using them for their own perverse pleasure. What was Mike like before he went to live with them?"

"He's sixteen now, was thirteen when he first came to live with them, and he'd already been suspended from one school, mostly for fighting."

"Any fire starting?"

"None until he went to live with the Hattocks."

"What do we know about Mike's life before?"

"Pretty typical stuff," Julian replied. "Dad was an alcoholic who beat his wife, he was in and out of prison. His mom was addicted to prescription painkillers after she injured her back in a fall down the stairs. Mike often went to school dirty and without food, teachers reported it to child protective services and he was removed from the home when they found out that the father had been beating him as well as his wife. He was nine when he entered the system, but because of his anger issues and his propensity to get into violent fights, he went through eleven homes in the four years before he went to live with the Hattocks."

"So why has he made it three years with them?" Abe asked, more to himself than to Julian. He hadn't interviewed either Mike or the Hattocks so he was having a hard time getting a read on the entire family.

"All the kids the Hattocks have cared for never showed any signs of physical abuse."

Abe knew that there were plenty of ways to abuse someone without laying a hand on them. While he and his brothers and sister had lived picture-perfect lives growing up, Meadow hadn't, and the psychological scars she had been left with had healed slower than the physical ones. He wanted to know what was going on inside the Hattock home and whether it had any bearing on these fires.

As he saw it, there were two options right now.

One, that whatever Mike Voight had lived through with his parents had left him with psychological scars, including the need to hurt others through fistfights and setting fires, and now he was out of control, escalating, and that meant that bodies were soon going to start falling.

Or two, that whatever Mike Voight had lived through with his parents was nothing compared to what had happened to him in the Hattock house. The two traumas combined had started this desire to set fires, and now he was addicted and would continue to escalate until people started dying.

Either option would lead to deaths and whether he had been abused in foster care or not, the boy needed help. Some of his anger toward Mike Voight had dimmed when he'd learned about the trauma he had lived through, but that didn't negate the fact that if he was indeed the fire starter they were looking for, he was one dangerous kid.

River's End was his town, his wife and unborn baby lived here, his brothers and parents lived here, his cousins and uncle lived here, his friends lived here, and every resident of the town was his responsibility. He had to find out if Mike was the man they were looking for, and if he was, make sure he was put where he couldn't hurt anyone else, be that prison or a psychiatric facility.

~

11:40 A.M.

Maggie didn't know exactly where she was going, she just knew that she needed a little time alone.

She'd waited until Theo had taken a phone call before quickly throwing on some clothes and writing a quick note saying she was going out for a walk before hurrying out the back door.

It was a coward's move, she acknowledged that, but she couldn't think clearly when she was around him. She couldn't think clearly while she was in his home either, it felt like him, smelled like him, and she saw him everywhere she looked.

What she needed was some time alone so she could figure out where her head was.

Her feelings for Theo were growing.

He wasn't just her friend anymore, he was something more.

Much more.

The more time they spent together, whether it was just hanging out playing video games, or eating meals he had cooked just for her, or having mind-blowing sex, it made them feel more like a couple. Theo's admission that he would take back sex with Amethyst if he could had gotten her thinking. Did that mean he was starting to see her as something more than a friend too?

She didn't want to get her hopes up, she knew that he was still hung up on Amethyst, and she was resigned to spending her life alone, so she didn't know why she was getting so caught up in this idea of her and Theo together. And yet although it made no sense, it was exactly what she was doing.

Daydreams of him knocking on the door, flowers and chocolates in his arms, to ask her out. The two of them on a date, candlelit dinners, picnics, skinny dipping in the river when the weather was warmer, celebrating holidays and birthdays together, going to bed together every night to make love and then fall asleep tangled in one another's arms. For some reason it was the falling asleep tangled in each other's arms that got to her the most.

She'd never had that simple intimacy of being held.

Not as a child with her parents and never as an adult.

It was something that she already knew from the one night she had spent sleeping in Theo's arms that was enough to keep the nightmares at bay.

Maybe that was the cause of these sudden feelings for Theo.

Or the fact he had saved her life.

Or the fact that he had been an amazing friend, offering her a place to stay and taking care of her.

Or ...

Maggie shuddered out a sigh. Did it matter why she was suddenly falling for her friend? The facts were that nothing was going to happen.

Nothing.

Nothing.

Nothing.

Why was she letting herself get hung up on this? Theo was never going to see her as anything other than a friend. The sex was only because he thought he was helping to keep her mind off everything else by making her feel so amazing that it washed all the bad stuff away.

It was sweet, but she didn't want pity sex, she wanted ...

Wait.

Was she really thinking what she thought she was thinking?

Sex to her wasn't the same thing it was to most people. Yeah, some bad stuff had happened to her and it had warped the way she saw sex, herself, men, and the world, but with Theo it was different. She had always known he was hot. He had muscles on his muscles, abs to die for, and that lopsided grin that had most women swooning at his feet. But she had never been most women, and while she'd known he had a hot body it had never done anything to her, she'd never even thought about so much as a kiss until he had been driving her home to his house.

Then everything had changed.

Unlike how Theo felt about sleeping with Amethyst—and probably how he felt about sleeping with her only she was too much of a coward to ask—she wouldn't take back sex with him even if she could. Those moments they'd spent together had been the best of her life, and she would treasure them forever.

When this was all over, when her hotel was rebuilt, and she had moved back home, when she and Theo had gone back to just being friends who occasionally saw each other around town or at a party someone was throwing, when she was lonely and sad and lying in her bed at night unable to sleep, she would relive those memories in her mind, and maybe she wouldn't feel quite so alone.

Alone.

She was so tired of being alone.

It was like her entire life it had just been her, everyone else was in the periphery, a part of her life, but not really a part of her life.

Theo changed that.

He'd just opened up his home to her like it was no big deal, he'd cooked her comfort food and he'd hung out with her, he'd taken off two shifts already just so he could be with her and she wouldn't have to be alone. How could she not be falling for him?

Once she went home though those feelings would fade.

They would, Maggie truly believed that.

After all, they had to.

She wrapped her arms around her stomach, running this over and over in her head was making her feel nauseous. She felt like she was losing her mind. These feelings were wrong. Theo didn't reciprocate, she was only going to get her heart broken, and it wasn't worth it.

It truly wasn't.

Just because she wouldn't take back what they had done didn't mean that she would say yes even if Theo did reciprocate her feelings and did ask her out.

She couldn't.

She had made a vow.

A vow to remain alone.

It would be wrong to break it.

Right?

She'd been too afraid to tell the truth, and someone had been hurt because of it, that meant she didn't deserve happiness. That was what she had always believed, but she had made that vow so many years ago. She'd been just a kid, and now, well, she wasn't sure exactly but maybe there was a chance she had been wrong.

She had done what she had to do, she just hadn't felt good about it.

Still didn't feel good about it.

But it was too late to take it back now, too late to do anything about it. So she should stick to the vow, remain alone, only she didn't want to. She wanted Theo, if he would have her, she wanted to see if they could build a life together, a life that could make up for everything she hadn't had as a kid.

Her feet stopped when her brain realized where they were.

The hotel.

She'd walked all the way through town, through the forest, and out to the hotel. Well, what was left of it anyway. It wasn't quite as bad as she had been expecting, the outside of the building was still there, although blackened in places.

The loss she felt when she looked at what had once been a beautiful, grand old building hit her straight in the heart like an arrow. This place had been left to her and look what she had done with it.

There were so many happy memories here.

This place had been her escape when she was trapped in the house with her alcoholic father and drug addict mother.

She had been twelve when she'd come to live here with her grandparents, and for the first time she had been happy. It hadn't been an instantaneous thing, it had taken time, a lot of it, but roaming the empty halls when there weren't many guests staying, and playing in the quiet forest, swimming in the river in the summer and making snowmen and snow forts in the winter. Bit by bit living in an environment where she didn't have to be constantly on her guard she had begun to relax.

Maggie smiled as she remembered Fourth of July barbecues on the lawn and Christmas parties in the hotel's huge living room, a fire roaring in the fireplace and mugs of hot chocolate with marshmallows for everyone.

This place had saved her.

Quite literally.

She had been safe here, protected, and loved by her grandparents. They had been patient with her, they'd never yelled if she spilled something or forgot to put things away. They had encouraged her to find things that she enjoyed and then work hard at them, that's how she'd learned she was good at music and started playing several instruments. They had expected that she work hard at school to get good grades, but made it clear that it was okay if she wasn't good at something, there were no punishments for bad grades if she had tried her best. They'd paid for her to go to college and then left this place to her when they had passed away a little over three years ago.

This place was the only home she had ever known.

It had been her sanctuary, her happy place, her safe place, and now it was gone.

Maggie dropped to her knees and sobbed.

~

1:55 P.M.

He was trying not to be hurt, and he was trying not to be worried.

Theo was failing on both counts.

If Maggie had needed a little time on her own she could have just told him, she didn't need to wait until he was on the phone then sneak out leaving a quickly scrawled note telling him she'd gone for a walk.

Two hours ago.

Where was she?

What was she doing?

It looked like the fire at the hotel and the explosion were indeed related, and that the one who had set both was a teenage boy who had been staying with his foster family at the hotel. That meant that this likely had nothing to do with Maggie, but until his brother positively ruled it out, he wanted to limit the time she spent off on her own, unprotected.

He picked up his phone but then set it back down again. It wasn't any use to him since Maggie's phone had been destroyed in the fire and she hadn't bought a new one yet, so he couldn't call her to ask what she was doing and why she hadn't returned.

When he'd first found her note he had assumed she was going to go for a short walk around the neighborhood and would be back in thirty minutes or less. But with hours ticking by, he was wondering if she had wandered further than he'd thought.

Or there was the possibility that something had happened to her.

This was River's End, everyone knew everyone, especially someone like Maggie who had been born and lived here her entire life. If she had fallen and hurt herself or been in an accident, she would have been taken to the nearby hospital and someone would have called to let him know. Since River's End was like any other small town and gossip reigned supreme, everyone knew that Maggie was staying with him.

He was worried about her. She was his friend and he cared a great deal about her, she was his responsibility, and he wasn't going to let anything happen to her on his watch.

Picking up his phone again, he scrolled through the contacts and called one of them.

"Hi, Theo, what's up?"

"Meadow, you heard from Maggie today?" he asked his soon to be sister-in-law. If Maggie had gone to see anyone or if anyone would know if she'd made plans it would be Meadow.

"No, should I have?"

"I guess not." Part of him had been hoping that Meadow would tell him that she and Maggie were hanging out together and that they weren't had his anxiety amping up several notches. Something was going on, and he intended to find out what.

"You guess not? Is something wrong? Did something happen?" Meadow sounded concerned now, and that was the last thing he wanted.

"No, I'm sure it's nothing. Maggie left a note saying she was going out for a walk and she's been gone a while so I just wondered if the two of you were together. There's nothing to worry about though, I'm sure she'll be back soon," he said, faking an upbeat tone he certainly didn't feel.

"Okay," Meadow agreed warily. "Text me when she turns up."

"I will," he promised. He didn't want his big brother on his case for worrying his fiancée.

Once he'd ended the call he grabbed his keys and went out to his truck. Looks like he'd resort to driving aimlessly around hoping he stumbled upon her. Anything was better than just sitting around and hoping she showed up soon.

As he started the engine, rain began to fall. Great big heavy drops that landed with a plopping sound on his windshield. Turning the wipers on, he began to drive, Maggie hadn't been wearing a coat when she left—he knew this because both the coats she'd bought were still hanging on his coat rack—so wherever she was she was getting drenched.

Theo sighed, wondering when he had turned into such a mother hen, worrying because Maggie was going to catch her death of cold. Of course he knew that wasn't true, you didn't catch a cold because you got wet, a cold was a virus, but nonetheless when something involved Maggie he worried.

A different kind of worry than he had felt for anyone else.

As a kid, he'd worried about his dad while he was in the military, and his mom had had breast cancer when he was thirteen. He'd worried that she was going to die and then he'd worried that the rest of his family would get sick and die as well. He'd worried about his team when he was serving, he would have given his life for any one of those men, and they had all at one time or another been injured.

But this was different.

This ran deeper.

The worry was a part of him, a physical part. It ran through his blood making it feel like ice and grabbed hold of his heart squeezing it painfully tight.

He was overreacting.

Theo was sure that he was. What were the chances that someone would have grabbed Maggie off the streets? Virtually none. She had probably gotten distracted, lost in thought, and hadn't realized how long she'd been gone.

The simplest answer was usually the correct one.

Although it wasn't a conscious decision, his brain—or perhaps his heart—seemed to know where it was going and he soon found himself turning into the long driveway that led to Maggie's hotel. While he hadn't thought about where he was going it was definitely the most logical of locations to start searching for Maggie. She hadn't been out here yet, and she was no doubt curious to see firsthand the damage done to the hotel.

There she was.

As soon as he stopped the car he saw her.

She was down on her knees right outside the large front doors, and even from here through the rain he could see her shoulders shaking.

Maggie was crying.

That about killed him. It wasn't that she didn't have good reason to be crying, she'd lost a lot and barely escaped with her life, it was just that her pain touched him. Really touched him. It was an odd and disconcerting feeling, and he was glad he didn't have any time to examine it too closely.

Jumping out of the car, he approached her slowly. She was upset and he didn't want to startle her.

"Mags?"

She didn't respond, just wrapped her arms more tightly around her waist and sobbed harder.

The sound of her weeping was worse than the sound of fingernails on a chalkboard. It cut through him as effectively as any knife could, and he found himself wanting to do whatever it took to take away her pain.

"Come here, sweetheart," he said, reaching for her and gently pulling her to her feet, settling her against his chest, her head tucked under his chin. He held her tightly, one hand nestled on the back of her head, his fingers tangled in her silky soft brown locks, the other hand alternated between stroking the length of her spine and rubbing circles on her back.

"It's gone," she sobbed.

"I know, baby."

"This was the only home I ever had. I let my grandparents down. They gave me everything my parents didn't, and look what I did to their beautiful hotel." She wept into his chest.

"You didn't do anything, sweetheart," he reminded her. He hated feeling helpless. Hated it. He'd rather deal with a gunshot wound than he would this feeling of being so out of his depth he couldn't fix the problem no matter how much he wanted to.

Maggie didn't seem to hear him, lost in her pain and sorrow. "I have so many memories here. So many wonderful memories of times with my grandparents and now they're gone and so is this place."

"No, baby, your memories can never be taken away from you. They're here." He touched a hand to her forehead that was dripping with water. "And here." He eased her back so he could press his hand to her heart. "Nothing and no one can take those memories from you. As soon as is humanely possible, we'll get your hotel back up and running. It's going to be okay, sweetheart, I know it might not feel like it right now, but it will be."

She looked up at him, her round eyes wet with tears as well as the rain. She choked on another sob, and then she wrapped her arms tightly around his waist and buried her face against his chest and clung to him.

"Come on, Mags, you're drenched, you're shaking, you're cold, I'm going to take you home, okay?"

She didn't offer an answer, but she also didn't offer a protest as he gathered her up into his arms and carried her to his car. He opened the passenger door, set her on the seat, grabbed a blanket from the trunk and wrapped it around her before buckling her in. Maggie had been the one to instigate the changing of their relationship, and he'd seen hints that maybe she wanted something more than friendship, but what if he was wrong? What if he was misreading the signals? What if he developed feelings for her only to learn that she'd needed him to get her through this rough time but nothing more?

That was a risk he wasn't sure he was willing to take.

2:17 P.M.

Maggie was shaking so hard her muscles ached.

Her wet clothes clung to her skin, the cold seeped through them and into her bones. Water dripped down her face, the droplets tickled as they trickled down her cheeks and off the tip of her nose, but she was too tired to bother lifting a hand and brushing them away.

The only sounds in the car were the chattering of her teeth and the blast of the heater. Theo had one hand resting on her thigh as he drove back to his place, it was heavy against her leg, and the feel of it was reassuring. Despite the fact that he had to be every bit as cold as she was because he'd gotten just as drenched in the rain, Theo's hand was warm, radiating heat that slowly crept around her body.

He'd come after her.

She hadn't intended to be gone for so long, she'd just started crying as the reality of everything that she had lost sunk in, and once those floodgates had opened she hadn't been able to close them. Theo must have gotten worried about her and gone looking for her, somehow figuring out that she was at her hotel.

Maggie knew how he'd found her.

He'd found her because she needed him, because her very soul had cried out for him.

And he'd come.

"Hey, sweetheart, we're here, I'm going to come grab you, just wait there."

The voice and the feel of fingertips brushing softly across her cheek startled her out of her thoughts, and she found Theo staring at her. She was more than capable of walking into the house on her own two feet, but there was no way she was passing up an opportunity to be cradled in Theo's strong arms.

Theo jumped out of the car, came around to her side, and when he opened her door he unbuckled her seatbelt, tucked the blanket tighter around her, and then scooped her up. It was still raining—hard—and by the time they got from the driveway to the front door the blanket was soaked through.

Despite the warm weather they'd had this spring the temperature had dropped today, making it feel like it was winter again. Maggie loved all the seasons, but right about now she was longing for summer with its endless blue skies, gentle breezes, and hot sunshine. In summer when it rained it was refreshing, but today the rain made her feel like she was an ice block.

Somehow Theo managed to juggle her in his arms and unlock the door without setting her down. Once inside, he closed and locked the front door then carried her through the house and upstairs to the bathroom.

He turned on the shower, adjusting the temperature until steam filled the air, then he turned to her and gave her an assessing once-over.

Maggie was just standing there, she knew that she needed to get out of her wet clothes but she felt heavy, lethargic, like every ounce of energy inside her had drained away and now there was nothing left. She was just an empty shell who had lost everything, and yet the man standing in front of her had the power to give it all back to her.

If she let him.

But she was afraid.

Her feelings for him were only growing, every time he was sweet and thoughtful with her it made her like him so much more, but she didn't know how he felt about her. He might regret that sex with Amethyst had changed their relationship, but he was still hung up on her, and even if he wasn't that didn't mean that he would reciprocate her feelings.

When he reached for her, Maggie felt her heart flutter in her chest. Did he have any idea how deeply he affected her? Just being in the same room as him made her stomach feel like a herd of hyenas had taken up residence in there. And when he touched her ... it felt like her heart had grown wings and taken flight, bringing her along with it, taking her on a journey through the stars.

Theo took hold of her hands and carefully uncurled them one finger at a time until she had released her death grip on the blanket. Then he grasped one of her hands and slid her arm out of the sleeve, he repeated the process on the other side, and the feel of his large hand holding her smaller one made her heart do a little pitter-patter.

She had it bad.

Sooner or later she was going to have to tell Theo.

Every second she spent in his presence her resolve to stick to the punishment she had given herself weakened.

Theo tugged her sweater over her head, then let his hands rest lightly on her shoulders. His hands were warm on her chilled skin, and when he trailed his fingertips down her arms he left a line of fire in his wake.

His hands settled on her hips, and he pulled her jeans down her legs. Easing her back so she leaned against the wall, he lifted one foot and slipped her sneaker off before setting her foot down and lifting the other, removing her other sneaker and then helping her step out of the jeans.

Although her skin was covered in a mass of goosepimples, she was glad to be free of the heavy denim, and the steam in the room was slowly warming her up. It was making her sleepy as well. She just wanted to curl up in Theo's arms, snuggled against his rock hard chest and pretend—even if it was just for a little while—that Theo loved her and was never going to leave her.

"Come on, you're half-dead on your feet, let's get you warmed up then I'll make some soup and tuck you into bed."

With a look on his face that she couldn't quite put a name on, he unclipped her bra, then slid her panties down. There was nothing sexual about his touch. It was tender and intimate in a way that was very different than sex but just as deep.

"I'll go whip up some soup, you stay in the shower as long as you need to, call out if you need anything." With that, he turned to head out the door but she couldn't let him go.

"Stay. Please," she added when he looked like he was going to decline. "I just don't want to be alone right now. I promise I won't try to seduce you," she said with as much of a smile as she could muster.

Theo smiled back. "If you need me, I'll stay." Quickly he shed his clothes, and although he had to be as cold as she was he didn't appear to be bothered by it. He simply hooked an arm around her waist and guided her into the hot shower, stepping in behind her.

As soon as the water spray hit her tired and aching body it began to work its magic. The gentle drumming on her muscles was better than any massage and a delighted moan tumbled from her lips.

Theo positioned her right under the spray and grabbed a bottle of shampoo, squeezing some into his hand, his long fingers began to rub it into her scalp.

She'd been wrong.

There was no way the water felt better than this.

Nimble fingers massaged her scalp and the ability to stand fled, she sank back against Theo, letting his strength hold her up. When he finished washing her hair he let the water clean the suds away, then picked up some body wash. Her knees went weak just thinking about how good his fingers would feel massaging other parts of her body.

In this moment it had nothing to do with sex. She didn't want to sleep with Theo, she just wanted to feel close to him, wanted something that went beyond sex, wanted something deeper, wanted someone who cared about her not for her body but because she was the most precious thing they had.

Fingers started working on her shoulders, kneading muscles she hadn't even known were tense and turning them into jelly. Her head fell forward as Theo worked his way slowly down her back, not leaving a single spot untouched by his magic fingers. She could feel his erection pressed into her back and knew that he wanted her, and as much as this wasn't a sexual thing to her if he asked her to, she knew she wouldn't say no.

But he didn't ask.

He just kept massaging her, down her back, then her legs, then each foot, her whole body turned into one quivering mess.

Theo had cleaned every inch of her, but instead of turning the water off he drew her against him, settling her in his arms, her front pressed to his. Maggie sighed a delighted sigh and nestled her head against his shoulder.

This was perfect.

There was nowhere else she wanted to be.

In this second, despite everything that had happened to her, she had everything she had ever dreamed about.

"Theo," she whispered, intending to tell him that things had changed for her and she no longer saw him as just a friend, but as the man she was falling in love with.

"Shh," he whispered back, pressing a finger to her lips.

Uncertainty replaced the feeling of peace that had been growing inside her, she wasn't sure if Theo knew what she was going to say and didn't want her to say it because he didn't want to ruin this moment by telling her he didn't feel the same way. Or if he just didn't want to talk because he was as caught up in this as she was.

Whatever the reason, Maggie kept quiet, but her grip on Theo tightened. She didn't want to let him go but she was afraid she wouldn't have a choice when this was all over.

~

8:31 P.M.

Maggie sighed in her sleep, her body wriggling.

Theo bit back a groan, not wanting to disturb her because she really needed the sleep but there was a limit to his restraint. He was starting to realize that Maggie didn't sleep much, no doubt the reason for the dark circles that usually marred the pale skin under eyes, and he wondered what the cause of her insomnia was.

She'd fallen asleep promptly after they'd had dinner—more comfort food, chicken soup this time—on the couch in the living room. He'd put on a movie, she'd said she didn't care what they watched so he'd foregone the chick flicks and chosen a horror movie—his personal favorite genre—and almost immediately Maggie had curled up at his side and drifted off.

Now her body was draped across his chest, her warm breath puffed against his shoulder, and her hair ticked his nose. One of her hands rested above his heart, and he wondered if even subconsciously she had put it there for a reason. Her other hand rested on his thigh, close—

painfully close—to the part of his body that longed to sink inside her and bring them both a world of pleasure.

But he didn't.

Because Maggie was vulnerable and she hadn't asked him for anything other than for him to be here for her.

So that was what he would do.

He would sit here, hold her, let her sleep, and keep his hands to himself.

Hard as it was.

And it was hard.

He had never used self-restraint more than he was in this moment. He wanted to grab her face, tilt it up so he could devour her mouth, drink in more of that intoxicating sweet honey taste of her lips. He wanted to tangle his fingers in her hair, and then let them roam her body, leaving not one part of it untouched. Then when neither he nor Maggie could stand it any longer, he'd plunge inside her, teasing her with his fingers, before he finally put her out of her misery.

Theo shifted uncomfortably, trying not to wake Maggie as he shifted into a slightly more comfortable position.

Not that one existed.

He was a glutton for punishment it seemed, he'd tortured himself in the shower, massaging every inch of Maggie's perfect body, and again he had used herculean restraint and didn't shove her up against the glass wall of the shower and take her then and there.

He deserved a medal for this.

Maggie shifted again, her fingers brushing against his hard length and he knew he'd reached the end of his rope. If he didn't take her up to bed now, he might actually wake her up and find out if she was up for another round of sex.

Theo wasn't sure what was happening to him. When they had slept together the first time he had known that it was a mistake that shouldn't be repeated, and yet here he was just a few days later desperate to make love to her again.

And again.

And again.

And as many times as they could before ...

Before what?

Until Maggie went back home?

Until she said that she wanted more than just sex?

Until she realized that she deserved more than him?

It was true. Maggie deserved a whole lot more than him. She deserved someone who could give her the whole soul mate kind of love that fairytales were made of. She deserved someone who would propose to her, who would give her kids, who would still be holding her hand when they were old and gray.

And he couldn't give her that.

Could he?

He wasn't sure and that in and of itself was an answer. If he wasn't sure if he could give Maggie what she deserved then he couldn't. And even if in the future he could, it was hardly fair for him to ask her to wait while he figured out his own tangled emotions.

As carefully as he could, he stood, scooping Maggie into his arms, and carried her upstairs. She was completely out cold, she didn't stir, her warm body just hung in his arms, feeling more perfect than it should. He shouldn't enjoy holding her so much, they were friends and he didn't want to go the friends with benefits route again. He wasn't sure what Maggie wanted and there was no way that he was going to let himself think anything beyond friendship unless Maggie made the first move and told him what was going on inside that pretty head of hers. And even then he wasn't sure what their future held.

All he knew was that the sight of Maggie's head on his shoulder was something that he could get used to if he let himself.

At the top of the stairs he stopped. His heart said to take Maggie into his room and put her into his bed, but his head reminded him of all the reasons why that was a bad idea and that putting her in the guest room was safer for both of them. He didn't want to get any more attached to her than he already was, and it probably wasn't wise for Maggie to get any more attached to him either. Her whole life had been thrown into a shredder, he wasn't sure that what she thought she felt for him was anything more than gratitude for him saving her life, and that wasn't a basis for building a relationship.

Guest room it was.

Theo carried her into the room and pulled back the covers with one hand while he balanced her in his arms. Then he laid her down and tucked the blankets up around her chin. Good idea or not his fingers moved to her hair of their own volition and he ran them through the silky locks. This would be so much easier if she wasn't beautiful, inside and out.

"Maggie," he groaned helplessly as he brushed his knuckles across her cheek. Then before he could do anything he would later regret, he quickly turned and fled the room.

It was still early, not even nine, but he didn't feel like watching more movies. Usually, he would have called one of his brothers or one of his cousins to see if they wanted to hit the gym or maybe go for a run, but he didn't want to leave Maggie here alone.

Unsure how he was going to spend the rest of the evening a glance down his body told him what he had to do next. Walking through his bedroom to the attached bathroom, not the one where he had bathed Maggie earlier because that would have been counterproductive, he headed straight for the shower. Leaving his clothes where they fell he turned on the water, then stepped under the cold spray.

Theo resisted the urge to move his body out of the icy water. He needed to let it do its job otherwise there was no way he was doing anything else tonight, including sleep. Although he figured there was a pretty good chance that by the time he woke up tomorrow morning, Maggie would have infiltrated his dreams, and he would find himself in need of another cold shower.

When he was able to move again without aching need flowing through him, Theo shut off the water and then stood in the bathroom wrapped in a towel, indecision filling him. He couldn't keep taking cold showers several times a day. He needed an alternative to working out his sexual frustration that didn't include Maggie.

Hanging up the towel, he shoved his clothes into the hamper, threw on jeans, a sweatshirt, and a pair of boots, then he headed back downstairs and out into the cold night. The rain had stopped, but it was still wet out, and he stomped through a couple of puddles on his way to the garage.

When he lifted the heavy garage door a smile lit his face.

This was the perfect distraction.

His 1952 Cadillac Eldorado.

He'd bought it when he first moved back to River's End, intending restoring it to be something to keep him busy and his mind off Amethyst. Now it was going to keep his mind from wandering to a certain brunette who was currently curled up inside his house.

Not long after his dad had retired from the military and the family had moved to River's End, his father had bought an old vehicle, and he and his brothers had helped him restore it. Those had been fun times, just the guys, out in the old shed down the back of the property, laughing and joking and working with their hands. Those were some of his fondest childhood memories, and he wondered if one day he would have a son and the two of them would enjoy times like this too.

Life had been busy since he returned, and between work and family, he hadn't had much time to work on the car, but Theo had a feeling that by the time the Honeysuckle Hotel was rebuilt and Maggie returned home that the old car would be fully restored and operational.

April 9th
10:24 A.M.

The library was quiet and peaceful, but it did little to ease her jangled nerves.

Maggie wasn't sure anything could.

Anything but Theo, that was.

But Theo wasn't here right now, she'd told him she wanted to spend a little time on her own this morning, and he'd said he had some errands to run but been vague about what exactly they were, so for the time being she was on her own.

Which was exactly what she had wanted.

Right up until the moment he had dropped her off on Main Street.

Then her entire body had screamed at her to stop him, wave him down in the middle of the street if she had to, beg him to stay, whatever it took for him not to leave her side.

She couldn't do that though. They were just friends, she had no right to act like a needy girlfriend, especially not after everything he had done for her.

Stepping from the friend zone to the lovers zone was a lot harder than it sounded.

It was a scary thing to know that if you made that jump, nothing would ever be the same, and that if it didn't work out, you would lose someone you cared about.

Too bad she was a coward.

If she wasn't, she would take that leap of faith, believing that things *would* work out and that she wouldn't lose something, instead she would *gain* something amazing. Something better than even her wildest dreams could conjure up.

But before she could even contemplate doing it, she needed him to give her even a hint that he was feeling the same thing she was. That he felt that same tug pulling them together, that his heart leaped every time they were in the same room, that every time they kissed he felt like the entire world stopped spinning and narrowed down until it contained nothing but the two of them.

Twice now she had gone to tell him that she was falling for him, and twice he had stopped her. It felt like a sign. A sign that things wouldn't work out between her and Theo and that she should stop living in this dreamland she had invented and give up the entire thing. She already had two strikes and one more and she'd be out.

"Hello, Maggie."

She jumped at the voice, then immediately felt silly when she looked up to see the eighty-nine-year-old librarian standing before her, a smile on her wrinkled old face.

"Good morning, Mrs. Hinton." She forced herself to calm down and offer the woman a smile. Mrs. Hinton had been the librarian for as long as she could remember, as long as anyone in River's End could remember, and the woman had also been a good friend of her grandmother's so she'd spent a lot of time around her as a kid.

"How are you doing, dear?" Mrs. Hinton's gray eyes crinkled in concern.

"I'm okay," she assured her. She wasn't, of course, but she wasn't going to admit that to anyone, not even Theo. Too many years being taught to keep things private was a habit too hard to break.

Shrewd eyes gave her an assessing once over, then Mrs. Hinton reached out a gnarled hand and clutched one of Maggie's own. "Your grandmother was a fine woman, a fine, kind, generous woman, your granddaddy too, neither of them would want you blaming yourself. From what I hear it was some good for nothing kid—an out of towner—who started the fire, no way you could have stopped that, dear. So don't you go blaming yourself, you hear, your grandmother would have my hide if I let you walk around thinking this is your fault."

She appreciated the kind words, she really did, and while she knew that she couldn't have prevented the fire, and that it wasn't her fault, it didn't take away the feelings of guilt that gnawed at her stomach. "Thank you, Mrs. Hinton."

The old woman sighed. "You don't believe me. I'm not surprised, I know how that family of yours messed you up."

Maggie sucked in a shocked breath.

She knew that it was common knowledge around town what life as a child had been like for her, but no one ever straight up mentioned it to her face.

An alcoholic for a father, a drug addict for a mother, dirty clothes, no food, left unsupervised sometimes for days on end when her parents were off on a bender, her childhood before she went to her grandparents' house was pretty textbook neglect kind of stuff. But it wasn't something she talked about. Ever. Because talking about it would mean having to admit the truth. And if the truth about her ever came out then no one in River's End would ever look at her the same way again.

"It's okay, dear, I know you had it rough, and I know your grandparents saved you. I'm sure you don't want to feel like you let them down, but let me assure you that there is nothing, and I mean *nothing* that you could do that would ever disappoint them."

Mrs. Hinton meant that to be reassuring, but it only made her feel worse.

She *had* done something that would disappoint them.

She had lied.

"Thank you," she said and hoped the smile she gave reached her eyes. "I was looking for some books on mechanics, car mechanics, you know restoring cars and things," she said, needing to change the topic before she turned and fled out of here in a flurry of tears that was only going to draw more attention to herself. As if she needed that, she was already at the center of town gossip with the fire, the explosion, and moving in with Theo.

The old lady nodded, but the look on her face said she wasn't buying the thanks and knew that the topic change was a way to wiggle out of the conversation. "Over to the left, right down in the back corner, you should find a few books there, if you can't come and find me downstairs."

With a last squeeze of her hand, Mrs. Hinton turned and walked toward the stairs to head back downstairs to the library's first floor.

Maggie didn't move until the old woman's fluffy white head disappeared and then she let out a shaky breath. So many things were swirling through her head, her grandparents, her guilt, the fire, the explosion, and Theo.

Theo.

He was at the forefront of her mind practically every second of every day.

She wondered if there had never been a fire if she would ever have started seeing him as something other than her friend. For some reason, the thought of never having kissed him, never having made love to him, never having been held so tenderly in his arms left her feeling like a part of herself had disappeared.

Suddenly ice-cold, she walked down to the area Mrs. Hinton had told her she might find some books on restoring cars. When nightmares had awakened her at three this morning she had tiptoed downstairs, intending to hang out there until Theo got up, but she'd seen the lights on outside. Curious, she'd gone out to see what he was doing and found him busy in the garage working on restoring an old car.

He'd told her how he and his brothers and dad had restored one when he was a kid and he'd decided to do it again. Immediately her mind had latched onto the idea as something they could do together. He hadn't invited her to participate, but if he was interested in it then she wanted to be too.

She was falling hard and fast.

It felt like falling into oblivion, into a hole with no bottom, but she couldn't stop herself no matter how hard she tried.

She'd known from the second she awakened the other night having slept in Theo's bed, wrapped in his arms, and made it through the night without a nightmare. Her grandparents had known about her bad dreams, they couldn't not when she woke screaming every single night, and had taken her to a therapist. He had suggested that she sleep in the same room as her grandparents. At twelve, she had thought she was too old for that, but her grandparents had insisted, and for a couple of months, she'd slept in a bed in the corner of their room.

It hadn't made a difference.

Over the years she'd slept in the same room or bed as others, boyfriends, friends on school camps, friends on vacations, but it never helped. The nightmares continued to find her every night.

Until Theo.

He was the only safe haven she had ever found, and the only reason she could think of for why that was so was because he was the one true love of her life. He was her soul mate, he was her other half, he was the man that could maybe find a way to put the pieces of herself that had been shattered—she had believed beyond repair—back together.

Theo gave her hope, he gave her faith, he gave her something to hold onto when her life had been a dark, lonely place.

He gave her a future.

If she wasn't too afraid to reach out and take it.

Maggie turned to face the shelves to start skimming through the books that filled them when she noticed something.

Smoke.

~

11:02 A.M.

"Where have you been?" Theo snapped at his brother when Abe walked into his office.

"Working," Abe replied dryly.

"On this case I hope." He didn't mean to take out his frustrations on his brother, but his instincts were saying that something wasn't right, that lingering feeling in the pit of his stomach that hinted at something bad happening. He couldn't shake the feeling no matter how hard he tried, and he didn't think it was because of the current complications in his friendship with Maggie.

"Do you really have to ask?" Abe dropped down into the chair at his desk and scrubbed a hand over his face. His oldest brother looked tired, and Theo wondered whether he had been working this case through the night. Meadow had gotten mixed up in this, and he knew Abe wouldn't stop until the man who had put his fiancée and unborn baby in danger was caught, and it was unfair of him to challenge his brother like that and imply he wasn't working this case hard enough.

Taking the seat on the other side of the perfectly organized desk, he rubbed at his tired eyes. It wasn't that he was unused to sleepless nights. There had been plenty of times both when he was serving his country and as a firefighter when he had stayed up for days on end with little to no sleep, but this constant worrying and turmoil and confusion was wearing him out.

"Sorry, Abe," he finally said. "I know that you're taking this case seriously, it's just that ..." he trailed off because he wasn't really sure how to finish the sentence. How did he explain everything that was going on between him and Maggie when he didn't even understand it? While he and Amethyst had never really been a couple he still felt like he was on the rebound, and Maggie had been through a traumatic experience and needed to feel like she wasn't alone, that was hardly the basis to build a relationship on, and that was assuming either of them even wanted anything long term.

Abe's assessing hazel eyes studied him for a long moment, and Theo was sure he was about to get a lecture about not hurting Maggie, since he knew that Abe and Meadow both knew that they'd slept together, but instead Abe went all business. "We have a suspect, a sixteen-year-old kid who was staying with his foster parents and foster sister. His name is Mike Voight, and he comes from a messed up family and ..."

Now it was Abe's turn to trail off, and Theo straightened in his chair. He knew that his brother didn't have to be telling him this, he wasn't a cop, he wasn't part of this investigation, and yet at the same time he was at the very center of this. He had walked through the fire at the hotel to rescue Maggie, and he'd been there at the car explosion. "And what?" he prompted.

"And we have some concerns about the foster family."

"Concerns?"

"We don't have any proof, but the couple has two deceased children and they seem to like to take on teenagers with traumatic backgrounds."

"You think that they're abusing the kids? That they killed their own children?" If this Mike kid had come from an abusive home only to end up in another abusive situation then it could definitely explain why he had turned to setting fires, it could be his cry for help, and despite the anger he still felt toward the kid for all the pain he had caused Maggie, he couldn't help but feel a little sorry for the kid.

"As I said, we don't have any proof, but it is suspicious and we are looking into it. As far as I know, there is no forensics right now that are going to help solve this case."

"So what's your next move?"

"We speak to the kids."

"Do you need parents' permission to do that?"

"Not if we speak to them purely as witnesses of the fire at Maggie's hotel."

"You think he'll slip up and confess?" Theo found that hard to believe but stranger things had happened.

"We spoke to him already but not the sister," Abe admitted.

Theo couldn't help but frown. "And the reason you didn't lead with that was?"

"Waiting to see how you handled the information," his brother replied evenly. "Don't want you going off and doing something stupid because you're personally invested in this case."

His mouth opened to deny that he was personally involved but then snapped closed again because saying so would have been a lie. Whatever was going on between him and Maggie he couldn't deny that he *was* personally invested. "So what did the kid say?"

"Nothing. He wouldn't answer any questions, was sullen, angry, but my gut says it's a cover for fear."

"Did you ask him if his foster parents have ever hurt him?"

"Yes, and he wouldn't give an answer."

"He didn't deny it though?"

"He didn't," Abe confirmed.

"If this was all just a cry for help, a way to try to get someone's attention so that they could help him, then why wouldn't he speak up when he finally got a chance?" Theo asked, more to himself than his brother, but Abe answered anyway.

"Fear can make people do crazy things. Like when Meadow finally escaped she wasn't ready to open up to the first person she met because she didn't trust anyone. It took time, and eventually she had to be backed into a corner before she opened up and told me everything. If he is afraid and he knows that he could get into a lot of trouble for what he's done, then maybe he's just not ready to talk yet."

"Even if this was a cry for help, he *is* still in a lot of trouble. Maggie's hotel was destroyed, and if I hadn't gotten to her when I did then she would have died." As much as he was empathetic to the boy's predicament—assuming that his foster parents *were* abusing him—it didn't make what he had done okay. Maggie and dozens of other people could have lost their lives, while it might get him a more lenient sentence, he would still be facing prison time.

"I think the kid knows that he's gone too far, and maybe it's not a cry for help. Maybe it's just taking out on other people, the anger and helplessness that the adults in his life have made him feel."

"You think you can get him to confess?"

"Honestly, I don't think the odds are in our favor. But we might be able to get the sister to talk. If we can get confirmation of what's going on in the Hattock house then maybe we can use that to convince the boy to talk."

"You'll keep me in the loop?"

Abe nodded.

"Thanks, Abe. Really," he added. He knew that Abe was giving him this courtesy not only because they were brothers but also because he suspected something brewing between him and Maggie. Before he could say more his phone buzzed, and he pulled it out. His stomach dropped as he saw what name was on the caller ID. "You got eyes on the boy?"

"No. I don't have the manpower to do that. Why?"

"Because we got another fire." While his brother muttered a curse and yanked out his own phone, no doubt to send a quick text to Meadow to check she was okay, Theo pressed answer. "What's up?"

"Fire at the library," came the clipped response. "Looks like it might be a bad one, we'll need all hands on deck."

"I'm at the sheriff's office, I'll be there before you guys," he said, already heading for the door, Abe on his heels.

Theo had barely ended the call when his phone rang again.

Maggie.

That bad feeling he hadn't been able to shake suddenly grew.

She hadn't said where she was going this morning or what she was planning on doing just that she wanted to get out, get some fresh air, and clear her head a little. He hadn't wanted to leave her alone, not after she'd gone to the hotel the day before, but he'd respected her wishes, he was hardly in a position to be demanding that she stay where he could keep an eye on her, and he'd taken advantage of the opportunity to come here and grill Abe on the case.

Quickly he pressed accept. "Mags?"

"Theo," she sobbed his name, her voice full of relief.

"What's wrong?" He froze, and Abe almost crashed into him.

"There's smoke everywhere," she said. He could tell she was crying but trying to hide it.

"Where are you?" he demanded. Was she in the library or was there a second fire that hadn't been reported yet?

"The library. I wanted to do a little research into something, and then I saw smoke. I tried to go back downstairs but there were flames everywhere. I can't get out." Her weeping became louder, and he could hear the undiluted terror in her voice. She had already been trapped in a fire once before, and that was no doubt compounding her fear.

"I'm coming, Maggie, I'm two minutes away tops, get as far away from the smoke as you can, stay close to the ground, and hold on. I'm coming for you, you hear me?"

"Okay," she agreed, and the trust in her voice almost brought him to his knees. She believed in him and there was no way he was going to let her down.

He didn't have a plan beyond running to the library, which was only a couple of streets over, and running through the flames until he found her and got her out.

Theo was already on the move, the same reassurances tumbling from his lips over and over again until he wasn't sure if he was trying to reassure Maggie or himself. "I'm coming, sweetheart, I'm coming, just hold on until I get there, I'm coming."

~

11:10 A.M.

I'm coming.

That's what Theo had told her and Maggie clung to that promise.

He'd come.

Just like he had come last time.

Theo had told her to get as far away from the flames as she could and wait for him.

She wanted to do that but ...

Fear was niggling at the back of her mind.

What if Theo *didn't* get to her in time?

What if something held him up?

What if he couldn't get through the flames?

What if it was too late by the time he found her?

Maggie was sitting huddled in a corner at the far end of the library's second floor, the smoke was getting thicker by the second and as it grew so did her panic.

She couldn't just sit here.

Ignoring Theo's instructions, she stood, swaying as the lack of oxygen made her lightheaded, and started for the stairs. She had to get out of here. She was going to lose her mind if she was in here for a single second longer.

Coughing as the smoke clogged her lungs for the second time in less than a week, Maggie stumbled and staggered as she crossed the large room, hoping she was heading in the right direction. Although she had been coming to this library since she was a little girl, the smoke and her fear were confusing her, she felt disoriented, sluggish, her brain didn't seem to be functioning quite right.

Was anyone else up here?

She hadn't seen anyone, but that didn't mean that there wasn't.

Maggie wavered.

The need to get out was overwhelming, but she couldn't just walk out of here if there was someone who needed help.

"Hello?" she called out. "Anyone here?"

Her ears strained but all she could hear was the sound of the fire that was quickly consuming the building and her pulse thumping in her ears.

With a sob, she resumed her fight to get through the smoke to the stairs.

Tears streamed down her face, and she wasn't sure if they were just because of the smoke that stung her eyes or because she was crying. She was so afraid she could barely make herself put one foot in front of the other. Why was this happening to her?

Three fires now in almost as many days.

First her hotel, then the explosion when she and Meadow had been shopping, and now the library.

Was she the target?

Were the fires because of her?

Was someone trying to kill her?

Before she could start worrying too much about that, she reached the stairs where an ominous orange glow met her. .

The fire was coming for her.

It was licking at the walls, curling out its fingers toward her. It wanted to take her, claim her, turn her into fire too.

Dizzy now, Maggie clutched the wall as she steeled herself and prepared to walk through the fires of hell. Anything was better than just waiting here for death to take her. She trusted Theo with her life, but that didn't mean he could get to her in time. She had to face facts, for now she was on her own. If she wanted to get out of here she had to find a way out herself. This time she wasn't just going to hide and pray that someone rescued her.

With her eyes stinging and her lungs burning, Maggie took the next step down the staircase then a rush of dizziness made her knees buckle, and the next thing she knew she was falling.

Right toward the flames.

Like they were alive they reached for her.

She fell in slow motion.

Her panic flared and then came a rush of acceptance.

She was going to die.

She had survived the fire in her hotel only to die in one days later.

Just as she thought that it was all over, strong arms suddenly closed around her.

Her vision blurry, her brain fuzzy, her lungs screaming for oxygen that wasn't there, she was too exhausted to see whose arms they were.

She was lifted, cradled gently, and then she was being carried back up the stairs.

No, she sobbed silently.

She didn't want to go back up she wanted to get out of here.

Back on the second floor she was taken over to the far corner—the very place where she was supposed to stay and wait for Theo—and gently set down on the floor.

"Maggie?"

She blinked and saw worried hazel eyes looking down at her.

"Theo," she rasped.

"I told you to stay back here, I told you I was coming," he said, his voice lightly reprimanding as his hands ran over her body from head to feet. "Are you hurt?"

"N-no," she wheezed.

"All right, let's get you out of here."

Without waiting to tell her what he was going to do, he snatched her up again, and then they were moving. The motion made her already pounding head spin so much that she felt like the world was actually trying to toss her off it. Closing her eyes, she rested her head on Theo's shoulder, trusting that he would know how to get them out of here before they died.

She had expected Theo to brave the flames again and carry her out the front door, but instead of the air around her getting hotter there was suddenly a rush of cool air against her skin.

Maggie forced her eyes open and was surprised to find that Theo had taken her up onto the roof.

"What ..." she broke off as she coughed and choked on the clean, fresh air, "what are we doing up here?"

"Not dying." Theo looked down at her and winked.

She had no idea what he meant, and right now, she was too tired to try to figure it out. She just wanted to close her eyes and give in to the exhaustion that lapped at her mind like waves on the seashore.

Sleep sounded so perfect right about now.

"Mags, stay with me, okay? I know you're tired, and I know you're scared, but I need you to stay with me, okay?"

"Yeah, okay," she agreed. He had walked through the fire for her once again, the least she could do was stay conscious. She coughed again and then asked, "What's your plan?"

"Them," he said when sirens filled the air. "You good for me to put you down for a minute?"

Although the last thing she wanted him to do was leave her alone, even for a second, Maggie nodded, and Theo gently set her down on the roof then ran over to the edge, waving his arms at his colleagues. It was only then that she realized he wasn't wearing his suit, he didn't have on an oxygen mask, and nothing was protecting him from the flames besides the jeans and sweatshirt he was wearing.

He had done that for her.

When she'd spoken with him on the phone, and he'd told her he was coming, she had assumed he meant he was coming in with his team, not on his own, unprepared.

He'd risked his life for her.

"Okay, sweetheart, it's time to get out of here," he said, kneeling beside her and brushing a lock of hair off her cheek.

"How?" she asked on a cough. Both floors of the library had to be an inferno by now, there was no way they could make it out, and it would take several minutes at least for the firefighters who had just arrived to make their way up here. Would the roof hold out that long?

"Down the ladder," he told her. "Can you stand?"

She nodded weakly and tried to control her coughing. It wasn't standing that she was worried about, it was the ladder. Did Theo expect her to climb down it? Maggie didn't mind heights, and usually she would be able to make the climb without a problem, but right now she felt so groggy that she wasn't sure she could do it.

Theo took her arms and stood her up, he walked her over to the side of the building where she could see the ladder raising slowly to meet them. "You go down first, I'll be right after you, okay?"

"'Kay," she agreed, blinking her eyes to try to clear the fuzziness.

When Theo released his hold on her, she swayed unsteadily and probably would have collapsed if he hadn't quickly snapped an arm around her waist. "You inhaled too much smoke. No worries, sweetheart, I got you."

Maggie didn't know what he meant by that, but she didn't have to wait long to find out. Theo lifted her easily and draped her across his shoulders, then he turned to climb over the edge of the roof.

Did he think he was going to climb down the ladder with her on his shoulders?

That was crazy.

Panic seized her again.

"No, Theo, you can't," she protested. She wanted off this building but not at the expense of Theo. If he tried to climb down carrying her he could fall.

"Don't worry, honey, I've done this before with people twice your size. Just hold on and I'll have you out of here in a jiffy."

Maggie clenched her eyes shut and curled her fingers into Theo's sweatshirt, clinging to him.

Somehow he made it down the ladder with both of them still in one piece, and she realized it had been silly to worry. This was Theo's job and she knew how good at it he was.

As soon as Theo's feet touched the ground he swung her around in his arms so he was cradling her against his chest. Paramedics swarmed them and with a sense of déjà vu that had both the fires melding into one hellish nightmare in her mind, she was laid on a gurney as medics fitted an oxygen mask and bustled about her.

Her gaze sought out Theo and she found him standing close at her side, their eyes met and she felt heat flush through her. This man was something else. Twice now he had saved her life. How could she ever repay him for that?

Theo reached for her hand and the second his fingers closed around hers, she felt that exhaustion come rushing back. She was safe with Theo, safe enough that she could let go. "Can I go to sleep now?" she asked softly.

"Rest now, sweetheart," he told her, leaning down to touch his lips to her forehead. "We're going to take you to the hospital, patch you up again, you just rest. I got you."

A smile quirked her lips up and comforted by Theo's declaration that he had her, she let herself slip away into unconsciousness.

~

2:49 P.M.

"Black."

Theo turned around at the sound of his boss' voice.

His boss' *angry* voice.

"Yeah?" he asked, meeting his lieutenant's gaze straight on, he had a pretty good idea what this was about, and he was ready to defend himself and his actions.

"You're lucky I haven't fired you or put you on suspension for that stunt you pulled today. Running inside a burning building without your gear on? Without an oxygen tank? Without backup? The truck was only a few minutes out, and yet you went in alone. You were unprepared and unprotected. What were you thinking?"

Simple.

He'd been thinking that Maggie was in there.

He'd been thinking that if he didn't get to her quickly enough she could die.

He'd been thinking that was something he couldn't live with.

"If I had waited a few minutes it would have been too late. I told

Maggie to wait in a corner as far away from the fire as she could get but she must have panicked. She was trying to get out on her own, when I found her she was at the top of the stairs. She fell, if I hadn't caught her, she would have landed in the flames. She was semiconscious," he said softly, "she would have felt everything, she'd have been dead by the time we got to her. An excruciating death." The very idea of the flames eating Maggie alive made him feel physically ill.

His lieutenant studied him for a long moment then gave a single nod. "Don't do that again."

Theo watched the older man disappear down the hospital corridor. He knew he'd gotten off lightly, not that he wouldn't have gladly taken the suspension or even being fired if it meant that Maggie had survived.

And she had.

Again.

Two fires in less than a week, plus the explosion that had occurred right when she and Meadow had been walking past the car. The explosion had been detonated remotely which meant that someone had waited until the very second that she had been beside the car before setting it off.

Someone was after Maggie.

He didn't need his brother to tell him that, he wasn't stupid, and whether or not it had occurred to Maggie yet, she was about to have her world turned upside down.

"How is she?" Abe asked as he came hurrying toward him. Abe had followed him from the precinct to the library and had remained on the scene while he rode in the ambulance to the hospital with Maggie. He had messaged about thirty minutes ago to say the fire was out and that he was coming to speak with Maggie.

"About as well as can be expected. Her oxygen saturation levels are basically back to normal and she can go home tonight, but right now, she's tired, and she's scared, and she'd hurting."

The look his brother gave him was grim. They both knew that if they didn't find the person setting the fires then Maggie would remain in danger and it was only a matter of time before he set another one. Sooner or later her luck would run out, and one of those fires would claim her.

Not that he had any intention of letting that happen.

"I'm going in with you," Theo informed his brother, arching a brow at him to see if he was going to refuse.

Abe merely nodded then brushed past him and opened the door to the room where Maggie was resting, and walked inside. She was lying on the bed, a tube looped across her face delivering oxygen to her lungs, damaged by the smoke twice so close together it was a miracle that she wasn't worse off than she was.

At the sound of the door opening, she turned her head. Her eyelashes fluttered on her cheeks before her eyes slowly opened. "Theo?" her raspy voice called out, a hint of panic.

"Right here, Mags," he assured her, walking past Abe so Maggie could see him, he crossed the room and perched on the bed beside her. She immediately reached for his hand and clutched it tightly.

"You saved me again," she said, her harsh voice nothing but a whisper. "I can never repay you for that."

"Repay me?" he teased, ruffling her tangled locks. "Why would you need to repay me? You know I'd do anything for you, sweetheart."

Something crossed her face, but it passed quickly, and then fear took its place. "Another fire."

"Another fire somewhere *you* were," Abe said, his hazel eyes serious as he pulled the chair over to Maggie's bedside.

"You think that someone was after *me*?" Maggie balked at the idea.

"Your hotel, the car right when you were walking past, and then the library while you were there," Abe stated the obvious because Maggie seemed to want to remain in denial.

"Coincidence," she insisted.

"We bought that after the explosion, but today changes things," Abe said.

"No, it doesn't." Maggie shook her head then winced as though it hurt. Given the amount of smoke she had inhaled it was likely she had a raging headache. "I wasn't the only person in the library when the fire started. And you don't even know that it was set deliberately." The last she said uncertainly like she wasn't sure that was true.

"Someone poured accelerant all around the library before they set it alight, Mags," he told her gently.

"But ... but ... I wasn't the only one there. Mrs. Hinton was there, and I saw a couple of other people there too ..." she trailed off, the remaining color on her face draining away. "Did they ... did they make it out?"

"Shh, sweetheart," he soothed, his thumb brushing across her knuckles as he held her hand. "No one died, they all got out. Just like last time it was you we were worried about." Maggie might not be ready to accept the fact that she was at the center of this, but he had and it left him petrified. How could he protect Maggie, keep her safe, when he didn't know who was after her or why?

"You're the only person, Maggie, who was at the scene of all three fires, the only logical conclusion we can come to is that someone is after you," Abe told her.

"No," she said firmly. "I don't believe it."

"Doesn't mean it isn't true," Abe reminded her gently. "Is there anyone you can think of who might want to hurt you?"

"No," she replied quickly. *Too* quickly. Like maybe something had occurred to her but she didn't like it. If she knew something she had to tell them. Just because she appeared to be the target didn't mean that sooner or later someone else wouldn't get caught in the crosshairs and wind up dead.

"Maggie," he started patiently because he understood that her accepting what was going on was beyond her at the moment, "someone has tried to kill you three times now. Just because they haven't succeeded yet doesn't mean that next time they won't."

She shook her head, her pale face, and huge brown eyes begged him to tell her that it wasn't true, but he couldn't do that.

Because it *was* true.

"Do you know anyone who has a grudge against you, a reason—no matter how small—why they might want to see you suffer? An employee at the hotel maybe? Someone who you had to fire who was angry, or someone who wanted a job who you didn't hire? Anyone you've had any trouble with? Someone who got angry with you over something, even something small like they thought you took a parking spot that was theirs? Any problems with ex-boyfriends? Or someone who asked you out who you turned down and they didn't like it?" Theo didn't like the sound of any of those options, but chances were that this was someone that Maggie knew, or had at least come into contact with.

"There's no one." Maggie looked at him helplessly. "No employees or prospective employees, no one I've had any problems with, not even anything small, and no boyfriends or prospective boyfriends. There's no one, nothing. I'm no one, why would anyone want to kill me?"

"I don't know, sweetheart, but Abe will figure it out," Theo assured her. He knew that his brother would work this case nonstop until he found the person who had been starting the fires, which now seemed to have nothing to do with the foster kid. Why would he want to hurt Maggie?

"If you think of something I want you to call me, okay?" Abe asked.

"I will, but I truly think you're making a mistake, this doesn't have anything to do with me."

"We'll see," Abe said noncommittally. "Why don't you get some more rest? Theo said you can get out of here tonight if you're well enough, so you should sleep."

Maggie nodded, her gaze immediately flipping back to his.

Reading the silent question he nodded. "I'll walk Abe out and then I'll be right back."

She nodded again, and once she'd closed her eyes he squeezed her hand and stood, following his brother to the door. "I think she knows something," he said when they were in the hall.

"I noticed that. She's scared, and she's not ready to accept this yet, but once reality starts to settle in she'll realize that this is real and she'll tell us whatever she knows. Why don't you try to see if you can get her to open up," Abe suggested.

"I'll do what I can," he promised. "Call me if you find anything out."

"Will do."

Once Abe was gone he dragged in a breath. Maggie needed to tell him what she knew, it may or may not have anything to do with this case, but they had to look into everything. Maggie's life was in danger and he hated that feeling of helplessness that came from not knowing how to keep her safe.

~

5:08 P.M.

How many lives did Maggie Wilson have?

He'd thought she'd be dead by now, but no, the woman was like a cat, she had nine lives. Three of those nine lives were gone now, the fire at the hotel, the explosion in Main Street, and the fire at the library, that left six to go, but he had a feeling she wasn't going to last that long.

He chuckled to himself.

There was no way that Maggie would survive five more attempts on her life before the ninth finally claimed her.

If he wanted to finally get her, he was going to have to adjust his strategy. At first he'd just wanted to kill her, something slow and torturous, something where she would suffer knowing that death was coming and unable to stop it from happening. Since that approach didn't seem to be getting him his desired outcome, he was going to try something different next time. Something a little more up close and personal. Who knows, this would probably end up being even better than what he had originally planned.

A slow Grinch-like smile crossed his face.

There were so many things he would do to her if he got her alone.

Maggie deserved knocking down a peg or two.

Or twenty.

Or two hundred.

She thought that she was so perfect, the sweetheart of River's End, the town's darling, the one everybody loved, the one everyone thought was just a sweet little thing who had never hurt a fly.

What did they know?

He and he alone knew Maggie's secrets. She wasn't the good girl she pretended to be. She lied, she meddled, and she saw nothing wrong with destroying a family so long as she got what she wanted. She had ripped his family apart without a second thought, sticking her nose where it certainly didn't belong, and convincing his wife to leave him and take their kids with her.

Who did she think she was?

She wasn't allowed to do that. She wasn't allowed to just do as she pleased with no consequence.

Well, she was about to come face to face with the consequences of her actions.

So the fires hadn't worked out, he had been disappointed at first, but now that he'd had time to reflect, he had come to the decision that this was better. He already had quite a few ideas of what he would do to her when he got his hands on her. He'd spirit her away, hide her someplace where no one would ever think to look for her so he could take his time with her without having to worry about being interrupted. Then he was going to make her feel every inch of pain that he had felt, her blood, her screams, her pain would ease some of his own suffering.

Now all he had to do was figure out how to make it happen.

It was going to take a lot of to the second timing, plus a whole bunch of luck.

From what he'd seen by following Maggie around town, she'd been staying with a firefighter called Theo Black. The man was the one responsible for Maggie surviving both fires. The firefighter had run through the flames to save her, and he wondered whether it was because the two of them were a couple.

Whatever, he didn't really care either way. The only thing that mattered to him was that the firefighter was also ex-military, and his brother was the sheriff, his two cousins were deputies, as was his best friend. All of them were ex-military, which meant there were many strong, tough, capable, alpha males circling around her.

Right now, he didn't have a plan of how he would get past them and to Maggie, but he was confident that he would come up with something.

At least he didn't have to worry about anyone ever looking for him, there was no way that Maggie was ever going to tell anyone about him because in doing so she would have to admit that she was a fraud. That she wasn't the sweet, innocent woman that everyone thought she was. She was a lying, manipulating, backstabbing egomaniac who thought the whole world revolved around her.

Every time he thought of her his anger bubbled.

And bubbled and bubbled.

If only everyone could see the wicked woman that lurked behind those innocent brown eyes of hers then the entire town would be better off.

Speaking of River's End, he was getting sick of this place.

Just a few days ago he had felt it charming and relaxing, the perfect place to hide under the radar while he waited to take Maggie out, but now he was just finding the place annoying. It was too quaint, too pretty, too perfect, it felt like a place that had been created just to taunt him. To remind him that the life he had lived was about as far away from perfect as it was possible to be.

He'd lived through hell as a kid but he had managed to make a life for himself. He'd had a job he loved, money to buy whatever his heart desired, a wife who was content to remain in the home, cooking and cleaning and tending to the children so that when he came home each night there was a hot meal on the table, his laundry washed and put away, everything perfect and in its place, the children fed and tended to and tucked away in bed where they wouldn't bother him.

He'd had it all.

Until he hadn't.

Because of Maggie, that had all been ripped away from him. His quiet, attentive, submissive wife had packed her bags and bags for their two daughters, and informed him she was leaving to go and move in with her parents. His daughters were ten and eight, tiny little things. They had worshipped the ground that he walked on and that his wife had denied him access to them left him fuming because he knew that their little hearts were breaking. They were missing their daddy, and he couldn't go to them because his witch of a wife had convinced a judge to give her a protective order.

Sometimes he really hated women.

They were wily, they were unscrupulous, and he used to think that he had found the one woman who was different, who was truly good inside, but she had fooled him, she was just like all the others.

When he was finished dealing with Maggie he would pay his wife a visit. Wisk her and their daughters away someplace quiet. A different place than where he would take Maggie, but somewhere that afforded him the same privacy because he had several lessons he wanted to impart on his soon to be ex-wife. Maybe he would even have his daughters watch, he didn't want them to grow up to be like their mother, he wanted them to learn proper respect, to learn their place in the world, and to learn that the world could be a dark, cruel place that cared little for them.

Kids should be taught that.

Instead, you went to school and learned that you had to make nice, you had to use your words and not your fists, you had to compromise, you had to share, you had to be a good guy. But why? That wasn't the hand he had been dealt, being nice, using words instead of fighting back, that hadn't saved him, it hadn't stopped anyone from hurting him. The only compromise he had been able to make was to keep his mouth shut so that he didn't heap more suffering on himself.

Why did adults lie to kids?

Why didn't they teach them the way the world really was instead of trying to create this perfect little fake world for them? Sooner or later they learned the truth, unfortunately for him it was sooner rather than later, but the truth came to them all in the end.

He wanted his daughters to know that.

While he hadn't raised them in the same environment that he himself had lived in when he was their age, he had made sure that they learned the same lessons he had. When they left home and went out into the world on their own he wanted them to be prepared, he wanted them to know what to expect so they didn't wind up hurt.

He had been a good father, he had loved his daughters as much as he was capable of loving another human being. He had been a good provider for his wife as well, she had never wanted for anything, he took her out for nice dinners and bought her nice jewelry, and how had she repaid him? By leaving him.

He placed the blame squarely where it belonged; Maggie Wilson.

And she would pay for everything she had done and then some, because well, he was angry and anger needed an outlet, that outlet was going to be the pretty woman with the long, wavy brown hair and the misleadingly innocent chestnut eyes.

Maggie was going to rue the day that she messed with him.

~

10:10 P.M.

Maggie yawned as she sat in the passenger seat of Theo's truck. She was tired but not sleepy, more like a deep-seeded exhaustion had settled into her bones, making her feel weary and like she was a hundred years old instead of twenty-seven. Part of the reason she wasn't sleepy was probably that she knew what was going to come as soon as she laid down in bed and closed her eyes.

Nightmares.

Horrific dreams of flames dancing around her, mocking her, laughing at her, trying to kill her.

That was something she wasn't ready to face just yet.

She suspected that she would never look at a fireplace, or a bonfire, or even a birthday candle the same way ever again.

Fighting back another yawn, she snuck a look at Theo. He was sitting in the driver's seat, his dark hair messy, lines of exhaustion written all over his face. Although he was focused on the road, he kept sneaking glances at her.

Worried glances.

It might make perfect sense for him to be concerned about her given everything that had happened the last few days, but she didn't like it. She wanted him thinking about throwing her down onto his bed and melding their bodies together in hours of lovemaking. She wanted professions that he was falling for her just like she was falling for him. She wanted kisses and hand holding and snuggling together on the couch. She wanted a date and maybe even a future.

Maybe that meant that she could let herself off the hook. It wasn't like she hadn't spent several years alone, keeping to herself, shutting people out, making sure she never let anyone get too close. She'd served her time so maybe she could parole herself, make an exception.

For Theo.

This was the second time in less than a week that Theo had driven her from the hospital to his house. Last time she had kissed him the second they got inside, and they'd spent the night making love, but she didn't think that was going to happen today.

That night had changed everything for her.

Changed everything for her but nothing for him.

Why was she even thinking about the future and the possibility of letting herself off for time served? Theo had made it clear that he only saw her as a friend and nothing more, that he wasn't interested in anything else, and she had to accept it. It wasn't like she was the kind of woman who threw herself at a man, especially when the man had already made his position clear.

She had to find a way to accept it.

Maggie just wasn't sure how.

What she was sure of was that staying at Theo's was hardly the way to go about accepting that the feelings she was developing weren't reciprocated. She was well aware of that and yet she had no intention of leaving. She needed to be around Theo right now, her whole world was spinning out of control and he was the only safe place she had, her own personal shelter from the storm.

"Mags?"

The voice tugged her out of her thoughts, and she was surprised to see that not only were they parked in Theo's driveway, but he had turned the engine off, walked around to her side of the car, opened her door, and was now peering through it, that worried look back on his face.

"You doing okay?"

"Yeah," she said and mustered a smile for him. Whether he liked her the same way she liked him or not he was one of her best friends, and she knew she was lucky to have him in her life.

"Let's get you inside." He reached over to undo her seatbelt, and she knew that he intended to pick her up and carry her inside. Maggie briefly considered telling him it wasn't necessary but quickly dismissed the idea. She wanted to feel, for once in her life, that she had someone in her corner, someone who wouldn't turn their back on her, someone who wanted to be there, who wanted to protect her, who wanted her to know that the world wasn't always a dark place.

When he scooped her up she curled her arms around his neck and rested her head on his shoulder. A contented sigh slipped past her lips before she could stop it but if Theo noticed he didn't say anything, just unlocked the door then locked it behind them and armed the security system.

That took the wind out of her sails.

Abe had said that he believed that *she* was the target of the man starting the fires. He'd asked her if there was anyone she could think of who might be angry enough with her to want to hurt her and she'd answered no.

But she had lied.

There was someone, she just wasn't ready to go there yet.

"You should go up to bed," Theo said, heading for the stairs.

"I've been in bed all day," Maggie immediately protested. "Can't we sit for a while?"

"Course we can." Theo smiled down at her. Veering off to the living room, he deposited her on the couch, grabbed all the pillows in the room, fluffed them up, and set them behind her, propping her up against them. "I'll go grab you some water and something to eat. Maybe some painkillers too," he added when he gave her an appraising once-over.

Pride had her almost telling him she didn't need anything for her headache, she wanted Theo to think she was strong, tough, unaffected by the fires and everything else that had happened, but that was silly. She'd already sobbed all over him when he'd found her at her hotel, and besides she already knew that Theo didn't think she was some damsel in distress who would fall apart just because she'd been dealt a rough hand.

"Grilled cheese sandwich," Theo announced as he came back into the room.

Although she hadn't thought she was hungry, the second the smell of warm cheese and toasted bread touched her nose she realized she was famished. "You really are amazing with all the comfort foods." She smiled as she took the plate.

"They're just what you need right now." He smiled back. Then he set the small folding table he had under his arm down beside her. He disappeared again, and when he came back he had a glass of water, bottle of painkillers, glass of orange juice, and a plate of cookies.

"Cookies are from Meadow, water is to keep you hydrated, juice to get your blood sugar back up, and the aspirin for the headache, you can take it once you finish your sandwich."

Maggie fought back a smile as she ate her sandwich. Since when was her big, tough, strong fireman such a fussy mother hen?

"How's your sandwich?" he asked as he spread a blanket over her legs and tucked it around her.

"Perfect." The grilled cheese wasn't the only perfect thing, but she wasn't going to tell Theo that. She truly didn't want to ruin their friendship because if being Theo's friend was the only way to keep him in her life then she would do it, it was better than nothing after all.

"You need anything else?" he asked, hovering at her side, clearly not done with the whole fussing routine. It was sweet, she liked this side of Theo just as much as she loved his playful side and his tough-guy side.

"No, thank you, this was just what I needed."

The second she was finished eating he spirited the plate away, unscrewed the bottle of pills and took hold of her wrist, lifting it so he could tip two pills into her palm before handing her the glass of water. Just the feel of his long fingers wrapped around her wrist made her shiver, she knew what those fingers felt like touching other places on her body and the memory of the times they'd spent together would be ones she would cherish.

"There we go," he said, sounding satisfied when she had taken the pills and drank half of the glass of juice and a cookie. "You're a better patient than I thought you'd be."

Maggie smiled, tired now, the sleepiness was starting to creep in, but she was afraid to go upstairs to bed and let the nightmares get her. She never wanted this moment to end, here in Theo's living room, him being so attentive to her and caring for her, she'd never had anyone do this for her in her life. As a kid, if she'd been sick there was no loving mom or dad to sit with her, hold her hand, hold her hair back for her while she was throwing up, or place a washcloth on her sweat dotted brow. There was no one to care about her, and that made her feelings for Theo grow once again.

"You want to watch a little TV?" Theo asked as he sat beside her on the couch.

What she really wanted was something she didn't think she could have, something she didn't feel like she had any right to ask.

"What? Something's running through that pretty little head of yours so out with it," he prompted.

"Well," she began slowly, "it's not really necessary, and you don't have to if you don't want to, really you don't, it's just that I, well, if you don't mind, maybe I could ..."

"Spit it out, Mags," he said with an amused smile.

"Do you mind if I sit on your lap," she asked, eyes down, afraid to be looking at him when he rebuffed her. "Just for a bit," she quickly added.

"If that's what you need after the day you've had then of course you can." His voice was warm, he didn't sound perturbed by what she'd asked, and when she chanced a glance at him his easy smile was firmly in place. "Come here," he said, sliding his arms under her knees and pulling her over so she was snuggled on his lap. He tucked the blanket back around her and then his hand on her head urged her to rest against him.

Happy to oblige, Maggie tucked her head under his chin and relaxed when his arms curled around her, holding her close. Tears stung her eyes, she wanted this, no matter how badly she thought she needed to be punished she wanted this, being held in someone's arms, feeling safe and protected, feeling cared about and wanted.

Not wanting to waste a second of being tucked up like this in Theo's arms, his breath warm on her forehead, his heart beating comfortingly against her, Maggie tried to push the sleep out of her mind and committed every single thing to memory because she knew this was an experience that would never be repeated.

April 10th
1:53 A.M.

Flames.

They were all around her.

She was surrounded.

They laughed at her, mocking her, teasing her, reaching out their fiery tendrils toward her then snatching them back just as she felt their burn.

They were closing in.

Any second now they would get her.

She had nowhere to go.

Nowhere to hide.

Nowhere to find safety.

They reached her, and she screamed …

Maggie woke with a start.

The same way she did every night.

Her sweat-dampened body shivered as the cool air touched her skin, she'd twisted and turned so much in her sleep that the covers were tangled around her.

Knowing that she wouldn't be getting any more sleep tonight, Maggie sat and then froze when she noticed the shadowed figure in the room.

Was Abe right?

Was someone after her?

Had that person found her and broken in here to get her?

Had they hurt Theo in the process?

Her fears melted away when the figure switched the light on and she saw that it was Theo standing in her room.

Those fears were quickly replaced by others.

Why was he here?

Had he heard her dreaming?

She didn't think that was likely because she had learned as a small child to keep her screams silent, otherwise she would wake up and *he* would be in her room.

Theo took a step toward her, hands up in a placating gesture as though her wild eyes warned him that he had to proceed with caution because she wasn't quite in her right mind at the moment.

"It's okay, Mags, it's only me," he said, voice soothing, as he took another step toward her.

"Theo," she said it on a shudder as she tried to pull herself together as quickly as she could. She wasn't used to an audience as she calmed herself down after her nightly bad dreams.

"You were having nightmares," he said, closing the rest of the distance between them so he was standing beside the bed. He reached down to untwist the covers, and she automatically shied away from his touch, she didn't want him to see her like this. Theo misinterpreted the move and his hazel eyes looked at her, offended. "I'm not going to hurt you, sweetheart."

"I know," she said, forcing herself to be still. "It's not you."

"The dreams," he said, tentatively perching on the side of the bed but refraining from touching her. "The fire?"

While the dreams *had* been about the fire tonight and the last few nights, saying yes to that seemed like a lie because usually her nightmares weren't about fires. If she told Theo that he would only ask her what the dreams were about and that was a conversation she didn't want to have. Hedging her bets and going with the half-truth, she nodded.

Shrewd eyes studied her. "The fire at your hotel, when I was in your apartment your laptop was on the table, you were already up even though it was three in the morning. You were having a nightmare that night too weren't you?"

How did he figure that out?

A lie was on the tip of her tongue all ready to slide out, but this was Theo and she couldn't lie to him.

"Yes," she said softly.

"That was before the fire so you don't always dream of fires. Do you have nightmares often?"

Again she wanted to hide the truth, tell him that it was just the occasional thing but she wasn't sure he would buy it. He somehow seemed to possess the ability to see right inside her mind, down deep into her very soul. "I have them every night," she answered truthfully.

"Every night?" He winced, and she assumed he had some experience with recurring dreams. "Mags," he said her name like he was sharing her pain and wished he could take it away.

She didn't know what to say so she just lifted one shoulder in a small shrug.

Theo shifted so he was sitting beside her, his legs stretched out on top of the blankets and he wrapped an arm around her shoulder, drawing her against him. Maggie hesitated for a moment then relented and snuggled closer, resting her head on his shoulder. She knew she should stop letting him comfort her, but she'd been starved for attention like this for too long and she just couldn't turn it down.

He began to stroke his hand up and down her arm. "What are the dreams about?"

Maggie debated how much to tell him. Since she had grown up in River's End, she knew that a lot of her past wasn't a secret. Everyone knew that her father had been an alcoholic who beat his wife, and that her mom was a drug addict whose only care in life was her next high, but there was some stuff that they didn't know.

Well, at least she hoped they didn't know.

How much did Theo know about her past?

He was only two years older than she was so there was a chance that as a teenager he hadn't really paid much attention to it at the time. There was always a chance that since his brother, cousins, and best friend were all cops that he somehow had managed to find out the truth about what happened.

A couple of minutes must have passed while her past and concerns over how much he knew had been running through her head by the time Theo spoke again, "Do you dream about your childhood? I know it was a rough one. Your dad was an alcoholic, right? He beat your mom?"

"He did," she whispered, scrunching her eyes closed as though that could somehow block out her memories.

"Did he ever lay a hand on you?" Theo's voice still had that calm, soothing tone, but since she was curled up at his side she felt his body stiffen as he asked the question.

Because this was Theo and she couldn't lie to him, she reluctantly replied, "A few times."

"It must have been a relief when he finally went to prison."

She'd been twelve by the time that happened, it had already been too late for her, but at least his imprisonment, subsequent suicide, and her mother's overdose meant she had gone to live with her grandparents.

Did Theo know what charges her father had been sent to prison on?

If he did then he was dangerously close to finding out she was a fraud, nothing more than a liar.

"Maggie," Theo said slowly like he didn't want to say what he was about to, "he raped you, didn't he?"

Her entire body clenched and if she wasn't so exhausted, and it wasn't Theo's arms she was wrapped up in she might have fled. Instead, she said, "I don't want to talk about it."

For a moment she thought he was going to push the issue and she honestly didn't know what she was going to do if he did, but thankfully his hand resumed stroking her arm, and he touched his lips to her temple. "You really have nightmares every night?"

"Yes. Every night for as long as I can remember." She wondered whether she should tell him and then decided she didn't have anything to lose. "The only night I haven't is the night after the fire when I slept in your bed with your arms around me."

Theo's hand stilled, and she held her breath as she awaited his response.

Was he going to tell her that he understood the significance of what she'd just admitted?

Was he going to tell her that he felt what was growing between them too and wanted to do something about it?

Was he going to tell her that he didn't think she should stay here anymore and he was going to find her somewhere else to stay?

In the end his hand resumed its path up and down her arm, and he said, "I'm glad I could help you."

Well, that wasn't what she wanted to hear, but it also wasn't as bad as it could have been. "How did you know I was having nightmares?" she asked.

"You've been up every night you've stayed here, I assumed you were having bad dreams about the fires so when I carried you up here to bed I decided I'd sleep in the chair so I'd be here if you needed me," he said, gesturing to an armchair in the corner that had a blanket draped over it.

Aww.

Her heart melted a little at that.

He was so sweet, worrying about her and sleeping here in her room in case she needed him. Surely that meant he felt something for her, it had to.

~

8:47 A.M.

"I win again," Maggie squealed delightfully as her Kart, driven by Princess Peach crossed the finish line in first place. "That means I've won nine games and you've only won seven."

"How did you get so good so fast?" Theo asked with a teasing grin. "When we played the other night I could slaughter you and look at you now."

"Told you I was a fast learner," she said, her grin wide and easy and warmed him deep down inside. He liked to see Maggie like this. Relaxed, smiling, having fun, all the worry lines wiped away, the shutters on her eyes gone. She was beautiful when she was like this. Well, she was beautiful all the time, but when she wasn't trying so hard to make sure no one got too close and she just let go, her eyes twinkled and her smile lit up her face.

What she'd told him earlier echoed through his mind.

The only night I haven't is the night after the fire when I slept in your bed with your arms around me.

Theo knew what Maggie was trying to tell him, that *he* was the reason she hadn't had bad dreams that night. That being in his arms was the safe place she had been craving her entire life.

But she was wrong.

He wasn't her safe place.

Well, he was but he wasn't.

He was her friend, and he was glad that sleeping in his arms had kept her nightmares at bay, but he didn't think that it was him personally who had done that. She'd been wiped out that night, she'd almost died in a fire, she'd lost everything, they'd just had sex, her emotions were spinning wildly, and she was likely just exhausted enough that she hadn't dreamed.

Although she'd been tucked up at his side when she'd told him about her nightmares and how she believed he had been able to banish them and he hadn't seen her face, he'd heard it in her voice. She was hero-worshipping him. She believed that he was her savior, and while he had saved her from two fires, that didn't make him a hero.

They were going to have to talk.

As much as he dreaded it because once they had that talk there would be no going back, Theo didn't see how it was avoidable. Maggie was seeing things that weren't there, letting her feelings get mixed up, confusing gratefulness for something more, and even though he didn't want to hurt her, he had to set her straight.

"Theo?" Maggie's smile had faded, and she was now looking at him with concern like she could sense what he was thinking.

Faking a smile he no longer felt. "Yeah?"

"What's wrong?" she asked, fiddling anxiously with the controller she clutched too tightly in her hands.

"Nothing," he assured her. Nothing except he might be about to lose one of the best friends he'd ever had. Maggie had written to him regularly while he'd been serving, nothing deep, just emails chattering away about the goings-on in River's End, books she'd read, movies she wanted to see, simple stuff that had helped to keep him grounded.

He wished that he had made the effort to help her in return.

Although he had long suspected—as had everyone in River's End—it wasn't until earlier this morning that he had gotten confirmation that Maggie's father had gone to prison for more than just beating his wife. Maggie had been sexually abused by her father, he'd bet his last dollar on it. As much as he would like to say that if she didn't want to talk about it she shouldn't have to, someone had clearly made it their goal to eliminate her and that meant that every single aspect of her life had to be looked into even if it hurt her.

And it would.

Knowing that Maggie was going to be hurt riled up his protective instincts like nothing else ever had.

The doorbell rang and Maggie's eyes darted fearfully in the direction of the door. "Who's that?"

"It's just Abe," he soothed.

"Abe?" she echoed, not looking anymore pleased with that notion.

"He needs to talk to you."

"Why? I already told him yesterday that I don't know who wants me dead."

That's what Maggie had said, but both he and Abe had known it was a lie the second the words left her lips. "I know you did, but we have to figure out who this guy is before he comes after you again and you're our best shot of doing that."

Leaving her sitting huddled on the sofa, her joy and excitement over besting him at the video game after just a couple of days vanished as though it had never existed.

"Morning," Abe greeted him when he opened the door.

"Morning," Theo returned.

"How's Maggie this morning?"

She had told him about her nightmares in confidence so he didn't want to mention that to his brother, instead he just said, "She's hanging in there."

"Good to hear," Abe said as he walked into the living room. "Morning, Mags."

"Hi," Maggie said, shrinking back into the sofa. "I told you I don't know who it is."

"You did," Abe agreed, unconcerned with Maggie's tone that clearly said she wasn't up to this conversation right now. "But I don't think you were being completely honest with us."

Maggie blanched, and Theo felt a growl rumble in his chest. What was Abe thinking, saying that to her? Didn't he know what she'd been through these last few days? Abe should be going easy on her, taking his time, coaxing information out of her not accusing her of lying.

"Ease up, Abe," he growled.

His brother ignored him. "I know you're scared, Maggie, and I don't want to make this worse for you, but the only way I can help you is if you're honest with me, if you tell me everything that you know."

"I don't know who it is," Maggie said in a voice that tried to be firm but failed. She turned scared eyes on him, and despite his decision to try to keep things as distant between them as he could, he went to her, sitting beside her and squeezing the hand that immediately curled around his.

"Maybe you don't," Abe continued calmly, "but I think you have an idea. An idea you're afraid to share. You might be right or you might be wrong, but, Maggie, I've known you since you were two years old and I don't want to see anything bad happen to you. If you tell me what you're thinking I can look into it, either prove that you're right and that it has nothing to do with this, or I'll prove that it does, and then we can put a stop to this before he comes after you again."

Maggie was wavering, he could see it on her face. She didn't want to lie to them she was just afraid and desperately hoping that this had nothing to do with her even if all the evidence was to the contrary. She was having nightmares before the fires even started, according to her she had had them every single night for as long as she could remember.

All the way back in her childhood.

There was only one thing he could think of that she would be having nightmares about back when she was a little girl. Her father had been abusive, hitting her mother and her as well. She had all but admitted it without actually saying the words that he had sexually abused her. Her father was dead, committed suicide in prison, but maybe there was someone else involved, something that tied the events from the past that she couldn't forget with the present.

Keeping his voice as gentle as he could because he knew he was asking her to relive the most painful and traumatic thing she had ever gone through, he asked, "Maggie, is there any way that this could be related to your dad and what he did to you?"

~

9:04 A.M.

Maggie's eyes flew to Theo's when he asked her if this could have anything to do with her father.

Abe's sharp eyes moved to Theo as well. "Maggie's father?" he demanded. "He's dead. What does he have to do with this?"

"Nothing," she said quickly. Why was Theo asking about her dad? Her father had died when she was twelve, a lifetime ago, and if it wasn't for those blasted nightmares she would have blocked every thought of him from her mind and her life.

"Mags." Theo's eyes commanded hers to meet his gaze and not break it. "You still have nightmares about it, every single night, but your dad has been dead for fifteen years, in your mind it's not over. Is it because there was someone else involved?"

She wanted to tell him he was being ridiculous.

She wanted to pretend that this wasn't happening.

But it didn't matter what she wanted.

Maggie had long ago learned that her wants and needs weren't important. No one cared what she wanted, no one cared about what she needed, no one cared about her.

If it was just Abe here asking questions then she might have lied, she might have continued to pretend that she didn't know of anyone who might want to hurt her, but it wasn't just Abe. Theo was here too and she couldn't lie to him. She didn't know why it was that he compelled her to speak the truth when she had been keeping these secrets for more than half her life.

Once she told them the truth, nothing would ever be the same again. She could stop worrying about her hotel being destroyed by fire because even once she had it fixed no one in the town would support her business. No one would support her either, she'd be an outcast, she'd have to move, she'd lose everything, and everyone, that she cared about.

But if she didn't tell them then she might die, and she didn't want to be trapped in another fire.

Damned if she did and damned if she didn't.

"It's okay, Maggie, you can tell me," Theo said, keeping her focus on him as though he sensed her inability to lie to him.

"M-my father, he, uh, he went to prison for domestic violence and child abuse. Child sexual abuse. Of me," the words tumbled out in a rush because she was afraid that if she didn't say this quickly she would lose her nerve and flee.

Theo still held her hand, and he squeezed it supportively. "I suspected as much." His voice was full of empathy, and she wanted to throw herself into his arms and let him soothe this all away with his lips but she couldn't do that, she had more she needed to say, and by the time she was done he would hate her.

"Was there someone else involved, Maggie?" Abe asked gently. "A friend of your dad's, maybe?"

"No," she whispered. She knew she had to do this, she didn't want to be some stupid young woman who kept secrets from the cops who were only trying to help her and wind up kidnapped or dead, but knowing it was necessary didn't make it any easier. "It wasn't my father," she blurted out, eyes still locked on Theo's.

Surprise flitted across his face, but he concealed it quickly, and the impossibly gentle look on his face broke her heart because in less than a minute the look would be replaced by one of revulsion. "What do you mean, sweetheart? You said your father was arrested for abusing you."

"I lied." Maggie finally dropped her gaze to stare at her hand resting in her lap. Theo still held her other hand, but he had relaxed his grip.

"Lied?" Abe asked. "Why would you?"

"Because he told me too," she replied simply, keeping her eyes fixed downward so she didn't have to see the anger in their faces. Theo and Abe had fought for their country, they had jobs where they saved people, they were men of honor and integrity, they didn't lie and send people to prison for things they didn't do.

"Who told you to?" Theo asked, squeezing her hand in a silent command to look at him.

Against her will, her body obeyed the order and found his piercing hazel eyes studying her. He looked confused, but he didn't look angry, she didn't know why. "It was ... it was ..." if she answered that question then there would be no doubt that she was in danger whether Abe was right about this or not.

"Maggie, the man who told you to say your father was abusing you, he was the one hurting you?" Abe asked.

She nodded miserably.

"Your grandfather?" Theo asked.

She shook her head.

"A teacher?" Abe asked.

Another shake of her head.

"You ice skated as a kid. Was it your coach?" Abe asked.

Maggie shook her head again.

"Mags, we're trying to help you here," Theo said, a little exasperation slipping into his voice. "I know this is hard, but whoever this person is might be the one who has tried to kill you three times already. Who is he?"

She'd come this far, surely she could give them the name. "It was Austin."

She'd dropped her gaze again, but she didn't have to be looking at them to feel the shock that radiated off them. "Austin?" Theo repeated incredulously.

"Your brother was abusing you?" Abe demanded.

"Y-yes." Maggie wished the floor would open up and swallow her whole. This was humiliating, and she knew that neither of them would ever look at her the same way again. And why should they? Now they knew her deepest, darkest shame. She had lied to the police, the court, and her grandparents and told them all that it was her father beating her and sexually assaulting her.

"Why did you lie?" Theo asked.

"Because I was an abused and traumatized twelve-year-old," she replied, her head snapping up. "Because my brother had been raping me and torturing me since I was eight years old and I was downright terrified of him. When my father hit me, and I was taken to the hospital, and they found evidence of sexual assault, Austin told me to tell them that it was dad who had done it and I was afraid of what he would do to me if I didn't do what he said."

That lie had been the turning point of her life. Her father had gone to prison, committing suicide shortly after, her mother had died of an overdose just months after her father's death, and when she had gone to live with her grandparents, Austin had gone off to boarding school, and she had finally been free. She had lied and finally gotten the one thing she had prayed for most of her life, safety. How could she not think she had to punish herself for that?

"My father thought that he did it," she continued because they may as well know everything, then they could decide if she was even worth the hassle of saving. "He thought that he must have done it while drunk and he had blocked it out and couldn't remember. He pled guilty, didn't want to put me through the trauma of a trial, then he hung himself just three weeks later. He couldn't live with what he did, only he hadn't done anything."

"Look at me, sweetheart," Theo said in that sweet voice of his that almost severed her heart in two. She wanted him so badly but she didn't think she deserved him. Powerless not to do as he asked, she did look at him and sucked in a surprised breath when she didn't see any anger in his eyes. "What happened wasn't your fault. You were just a child. And your dad *did* hurt you."

She shrugged like that didn't matter.

Because it didn't.

Her father *had* hit her many times, but that didn't mean she could accuse him of something so awful.

"I could have told the truth, I could have told them what Austin was doing to me, but I didn't. Lying might have been Austin's idea, but I went along with it and because of that my father died. His death is on me."

"No," Theo said firmly.

"Yes," she shot back just as firmly. "Austin said his death was my fault and he was right."

"That was just him trying to control you, continuing to mess with your head so he could keep you under his thumb," Theo lectured.

"No it wasn't," she countered. "My father left me a note, apologizing for what he did and telling me he couldn't live with knowing he had done that to me. He killed himself because of my lie."

"*Austin's* lie," Theo corrected.

She wasn't going to sit here and play semantics with him. In her father's own words, he had killed himself because of what he thought he had done, he thought he had done it because she'd told him he had, as far as she was concerned that put the blame squarely on her shoulders.

"Why would Austin try to hurt you now?" Abe asked, stopping her from reiterating her role in her father's death.

"Because his life is falling apart, because of me."

"What happened?"

"Austin is married, he has two little girls." Again she felt, rather than saw the Black brothers' horrified expressions, the same horror she had felt when she learned her brother was married and expecting a daughter. She knew what was going to happen to that little girl, the same thing that had happened to her. "I told his wife as soon as the baby was born, but she didn't believe me. There was nothing else I could do, I couldn't force her to leave him. If I'd told her the truth maybe it would have changed something, but I was scared, and I didn't have any proof. Austin can be charming and my father was already on record as being the man who abused me, so I just stayed away from them, I couldn't bear to watch those little girls suffer the same things I did."

It was the coward's route, she accepted that.

"Something changed though," Abe said.

She nodded her confirmation. "His wife came to me after she found bloody sheets in her eight-year-old's room. She was distraught, she wished she had believed me, she blamed herself for what happened to her girls, but it was …" she trailed off because she knew that Theo and Abe would be thinking the same thing she was. It was her fault what had happened to her nieces, if she had been honest then Austin might have been sent to prison and they would never have been hurt.

"She left him?" Abe asked.

"And took the girls. She's filed for divorce, and she got a protective order so he can't go near her or her daughters. Austin blames me, and while I want to say he would never try to burn me alive he's sadistic and egocentric, and since he thinks I'm the cause of him losing his family then …" she trailed off not needing to finish the sentence.

She was an expert at making a mess not only of her own life but of the lives of everyone around her.

Is that what she would do to Theo if they became a couple?

Her eyes lifted to find his staring at her like he was trying to figure out what was running through her head. She was sure she had lost any chance of them being together now he knew the truth about her, but she had to know for sure.

Maggie was tired of hiding.

She had finally admitted the truth and regardless of the consequences—possibly legal ones since she had lied under oath—she was glad that it was finally out in the open.

It felt freeing, like a huge weight had been lifted off her shoulders.

Emboldened now she knew what she had to do, she had to confront Theo head-on about the energy buzzing between them.

The worst he could do was turn her down, and what was one more loss when she had already lost so much?

~

9:40 A.M.

He wanted to say something, do something, to make the pain and guilt in Maggie's eyes go away.

Logically, Theo knew that there was no magic pill, Austin had really done a number with his sister's head, and she had been living with the guilt of the lie he forced her to tell for so long that it wasn't going to go away overnight. The best he could hope was that now she had finally told someone the weight of carrying around the secret would slowly lift off her shoulders, and one day she might recognize things for the way they were. Austin had used and abused her, and if she hadn't agreed to do as he told her then the reality was he probably would have killed her.

Since he couldn't think of anything helpful enough to say, he didn't say anything, and Maggie finally looked away from him. He felt the loss like a physical ache, and he debated for the hundredth time since the first fire what was so bad about going the whole friends to lovers thing.

"Maggie, do you know where Austin is?" Abe asked.

"No, I haven't spoken to him since our grandparents' funeral, and that was six years ago. I, uh, try to stay away from him as much as possible." She shivered, and he assumed it was an involuntary action as she thought of the hell he had put her through.

Theo ached to pull her into his arms, comfort her, kiss her, or make love to her if that was what it took to make her forget just for a little while all the horrible things Austin had done to her. But once again he didn't. He couldn't. He couldn't have it both ways, he couldn't keep comforting her and taking care of her and then at the same time, tell her that there would never be anything more between them than friendship.

"Abe?" Maggie asked, her voice suddenly sounded very young and scared. "Am I going to be charged with something for lying about my dad?"

His brother reached over and took Maggie's free hand—because Theo still clutched her other and couldn't let it go no matter how much his brain told him he should. "No, sweetheart. You were intimidated into making that complaint, and I doubt any DA in the country would prosecute you for perjury when you were an abused and coerced twelve-year-old child."

"But my father died because of that lie. Isn't that some sort of manslaughter or something?" she pressed, clearly not convinced.

"If anyone is responsible for that, it's Austin," Theo growled. What he wouldn't give to get his hands on the man. Growing up, Austin had been a couple of years older than him, the same age as his brother Levi, but River's End was a small town where everyone knew everyone else, and they had played together as children. There had always been something about Austin that hadn't sat well with him, he was too charming, too in control, too carefully calm no matter what happened.

"Really, Maggie, I promise, no charges will be filed," Abe promised her.

"What about the boy?" Maggie asked. "The one you thought might have set the fire at my hotel and caused the explosion, this could still be him, couldn't it?"

"No, I'm sorry, he has an alibi for the fire at the library," Abe told her gently. "And we finally got his sister to talk. The foster parents were abusing them, made them sleep in cages in the basement, made them cook and clean, barely fed them, and made them do some sexual stuff to each other. The kid was just angry and hurting and trying to get someone's attention, trying to see if anyone cared about what was happening to him. He didn't do this, Maggie, but it sounds like Austin has a motive to hurt you."

She nodded glumly and exhaustion rolled off her in waves. Not only had she lived through indescribable horror as a child, but the stress of the last week was taking a toll on her, and finding out it linked back to that horrific past was a blow she didn't need right now.

"I'm going to go, see what I can find out about what Austin has been up to since he left River's End. Why don't you get some rest, Mags? I'm going to have more questions for you later," Abe warned as he released her hand and stood.

Theo stood too and walked his brother to the door. "The kid really out as a suspect?" he asked quietly.

"Yes, Will had eyes on him when the library fire was started, and the sister told us everything, the boy confirmed it once we told him what we knew."

"So this really is about Maggie, and it probably really is her brother, angry that she caused his family to fall apart." Maggie had been through enough and he hated that she was once again in danger.

"We'll do everything we can to find Austin and end this ASAP," Abe promised.

He knew that his brother would, but that didn't guarantee that they would find Austin before he came after Maggie again. There were no guarantees that anyone could protect her and that made him feel ill.

"You should go grab some sleep," he told Maggie when he closed and locked the door, setting the alarm, and praying it was enough to keep her safe. If it came down to it, he would protect Maggie with his dying breath, but Austin was smart, charming, and cunning. He had abused his sister for years, no doubt his wife and daughters too. He was accustomed to getting what he wanted, and right now what he wanted was Maggie.

Well, he couldn't have her.

Because she was his.

"No," she said firmly. "We need to talk."

"We can talk later," he said. That sudden burst of possessiveness was washed away by his desire not to repeat past mistakes.

"No," she said again. "We need to do this now, I'm tired of running away from things."

There was a fire in her eyes that hadn't been there before. He had always known that Maggie was strong, even when he'd thought all she had survived was alcohol and drug use in the home and domestic violence, but now he knew the extent of her suffering he thought she was one of the strongest people he'd ever met. This was different, this was a confidence that hadn't been there before, a determination that said she was going to go after what she wanted.

He acquiesced with a nod and sat down in the armchair, trying to force his tense body to relax. The look she gave him said she saw through his charade, but she didn't address it or beat around the bush. "I like you as more than a friend. Since the fire, since that night we spent together, I've been developing feelings for you, feelings that go beyond friendship. I need to know where you stand."

Her bluntness surprised him, and the poised way she held herself and his gaze made him respect her even more, and damn if it didn't make her even sexier. Hurting her just got even harder. "Maggie," he began slowly, "we're friends, I don't think we should do anything that would risk that."

"So you don't feel the same way?" she asked, not letting him off the hook with his vague answer.

"No," he replied, unsure if he was lying or being truthful.

She studied him for a moment before speaking again, "So, what? Because Amethyst chose someone else you're going to remain alone for the rest of your life? That seems like a waste."

"It's not just Amethyst," he protested. One strike and he probably would have been game to do the friends having sex thing again, but he was already on strike two. He hadn't intended to tell her anything more, but the patient way she stared him down had him talking anyway. "When I was serving in the Marines there was a girl. I was in a no-combat zone, she was there giving humanitarian aid, we were friends, and then we were friends with benefits. The threat level escalated, she was supposed to get out but she wouldn't leave, she got herself taken hostage and they ... they did some bad stuff to her," he finished softly, not wanting to dredge up old memories of what Talia had looked like when he'd found her.

"You saved her," Maggie said, equally as softly.

"Yeah, and when I did I realized I felt more for her than I thought I did. She wasn't just a friend to me anymore. But she didn't feel the same way. There was a guy back home who she had ended things with because he thought it was too dangerous for her to be doing what she did. She said those days she was held prisoner, being tortured, she realized that she loved him. She went back to him, last I heard they'd just had their third kid. I'm not stupid enough to try the friends and sex thing again, Mags, it never works, someone always wants more, and I don't want to get hurt again."

"I get where you're coming from, but *I'm* the one who's saying they have feelings, so *I'm* the one who stands to get hurt."

Trying to keep his voice as kind as possible, he said, "Mags, these feelings that you think you have for me, they're probably just because I'm the one who pulled you out of the fire. I think that you've latched onto me because of that, but honestly, it could have been any one of us who went for you that night. I care about you a lot, and I love you as a friend, but these feelings you have for me aren't real, they'll fade once we find your brother and you're safe and your life goes back to normal."

"Well, if that isn't the most condescending thing I've ever heard you say." She sounded more disappointed in him than angry with him. "So you know how I feel now, do you?"

"I just don't want to hurt you," he implored, begging her to understand that if he took this leap of faith and Maggie realized that what he'd just told her was true and that she didn't really feel anything for him beyond friendship, then he was the one who would be hurt.

No.

Not hurt.

Crushed.

"I think maybe it would be best if I moved out," Maggie announced.

"What?" He shot upright in his chair, that wasn't what he wanted.

"I know how I feel, Theo, whether you want to believe it or not. And if you don't feel the same way—or you're too afraid to admit that you do—then I *am* going to wind up hurt staying here."

What could he say to that?

She was right.

As much as he didn't want to, he couldn't ask her to stay because he was selfish enough to want to keep her close while offering her nothing in return, so he slowly nodded. "Okay, I think you're right."

Maggie's gaze bore into him as though she were trying to see deep down into his mind to determine if he really meant what he'd just said. She must have determined that he did because with a disappointed sigh, she stood and walked upstairs.

~

3:11 P.M.

"You don't have to go."

Maggie stopped what she was doing to look over at Theo, shooting a look that said he was being either delusional or extremely naïve. "Of course I do."

This wasn't how she had hoped this would turn out. When she

confronted Theo and told him how she felt, she had hoped it would prod him into setting aside his fears and admitting that he liked her too.

Theo was afraid.

She got that.

She *really* did.

If anyone knew about being afraid it was her. She had been afraid every single day living in her house. If it wasn't her mother screaming at them all in her hysterical manner, or her father throwing furniture or putting holes in the walls or beating her or her mom, it was her brother hitting her or breaking her bones or sneaking into her room after their parents passed out. Even after she had gone to live with her grandparents she had been afraid that someone would find out that she had lied and not only would she be in trouble with the law, but Austin would be furious and come for her.

She had let her fear of Austin keep her from living her life. Maggie couldn't say that she would ever not feel responsible for her father's death, and she would always be affected by the horrible things that her brother had done to her, but finally telling the truth had made her realize that she wanted a life.

A real life, the kind of life everyone else had.

She wanted to fall in love, get married, and have a family of her own, the kind of family she had dreamed about as a kid. It would be hard, she was under no illusions of that. She had scars that ran deep, and it was terrifying to even think of moving on with her life because as weird as it was, there was an odd kind of safety in living in the same little bubble she had locked herself into.

So while she understood that accepting that she liked him was a big step for Theo, he'd done the whole friends to lovers thing twice before and both times he had been burned, he was missing out on something good by letting fear dictate his life.

Just like she had done.

She had let fear of Austin dictate every choice she made. She let it keep her distant from everyone, she turned down potential suitors, she kept friends at arms-length, and she'd been lonely and hurting.

For her, that had all changed when she woke up in Theo's arms and realized she had had her first night's sleep that she could remember that wasn't plagued with nightmares.

What would be Theo's turning point?

What would be the one thing that made him realize what he wanted?

And would it be too late by then?

For them she feared it would be.

Maggie had the feeling that if she walked out of Theo's house then any chance they might have had at being a couple would be gone. Forever.

A couple of hours had passed since she had said it might be best if she left and Theo had agreed. In that time, she had come up to the spare bedroom, she'd made some phone calls, speaking with the insurance company, touching base with a few construction companies, organizing getting a new license, hiring a rental car, she wanted control of her life back. She was sick of spinning in circles like she wasn't tethered to anything, she didn't want to just drift through life anymore. She had come face to face with her own mortality twice this past week, and it had taught her that life could be gone in a split second, and that had made her realize just how much she wanted to live.

"Mags?" Theo had crossed the room and was standing beside her as she stood next to the bed folding clothes and packing them into a suitcase.

"What?"

"You really don't have to leave." His tone was imploring like he wanted to beg her to stay, but he didn't have to beg. All he had to do was ask her to stay and she would. She *wanted* to stay, she just wasn't a masochist. She had gone through enough in her life, been hurt by enough people, she wasn't going to put herself in a position to be hurt again, and if Theo couldn't accept that something was growing between them then he *would* end up hurting her.

"We've been over this," she reminded him, not stopping from her task, if she let herself drown in those gorgeous eyes of his then she feared she would cave and stay. "You know how I feel, I haven't hidden it from you, I came right out and told you. You said you don't feel the same way, and you also said that you don't want to hurt me. If I stay I'll get hurt.

Has anything changed?" It wasn't enough to just say stay, the stay had to be because he wanted more than just friendship with her.

Theo looked like he was waging an internal war, but eventually he shook his head. "No, nothing has changed."

Every time he said that it was like he stuck another knife into her heart. This was the flip side to letting people into her life, she gave them the ability to cause her pain. While she knew that Theo would never lay a hand on her like her father and brother had, she also knew that he possessed the ability to shatter her heart into a million pieces like no one else could.

"Then I have to leave," she said. The pain on his face almost made her take the words back, she didn't want to hurt him, but she had to finally place some value on herself.

"But, Maggie—"

"No," she cut him off firmly, "no buts. You only see us as friends, I want more, which means that this isn't the place for me."

"So where are you going to go?" he demanded. "You know that your brother is after you. It's not safe for you to be staying alone."

"Who said anything about staying alone?" She wasn't stupid and she didn't have a death wish. She had finally decided that lies or not, bad decisions or not, it wasn't too late for her to have a life, she wasn't going to hand it over to someone else so soon. Especially not to her brother.

"Then where are you staying?" he asked suspiciously. "With Abe and Meadow?"

She'd thought about it, but her brother enjoyed hurting people. While he preferred to manipulate and terrorize the vulnerable people in his family who he had access to without anyone knowing, he had already proved he wasn't above putting others in danger to get to her, so there was no way she would stay with her seven months pregnant friends. "No, not with Abe and Meadow."

"Then who? You're not going to go and do something stupid like stay alone in a hotel, are you?"

"Stupid?" she repeated, offended. "When do I ever do something stupid?" She had to be one of the most sensible people on the planet.

"Then who are you staying with?" he asked for the third time.

Closing the suitcase, she was just zipping it up when a horn beeped outside. Since she hadn't answered his question he raised a brow at her and stalked over to the window, shifting the curtains so he could see who was in his driveway.

"Fletcher? You're staying with Fletcher?" His eyes were wide and disbelieving when he spun back around to face her.

"What's wrong with that?" she asked, setting the suitcase on the floor and rolling it toward the door. "Fletcher is a cop, I'll be safe with him, and I've known him even longer than I've known you so I still get to stay with a friend."

Although she had turned her back and started for the stairs, she could feel his frustration. Fletcher was Theo's best friend and a total ladies' man. Maggie wasn't sure she remembered him dating anyone for more than a couple of weeks, tops. But he was a good guy, sweet, charming, fun, and she would feel safe with him which right now was number one on her list.

It wasn't that she'd called Fletcher and asked if she could stay with him to make Theo jealous, and yet ...

Okay, maybe that had been part of it.

As she dragged her suitcase down the stairs the first inclination that Theo wasn't going to back down started to gnaw at her. It wasn't like she was trying to bluff him, but part of her had hoped that when he realized she was serious about leaving he would realize he couldn't let her go.

Ask me to stay.

Ask me to stay.

Ask me to stay.

Maggie repeated the mantra as she walked down the front path toward Fletcher's truck.

All afternoon she had wished that Theo would stop her, tell her that he didn't just want her to stay because he was being possessive, but because that possessiveness meant something deeper. Something perhaps he was too afraid to even admit yet.

But he didn't ask her to stay.

Instead, he stood in the doorway watching with a glower as Fletcher took her suitcase and then helped her up into the passenger seat, his lips pressed stubbornly into a thin line. As Fletcher drove away, she had to admit that maybe she had been wrong about Theo, maybe he really didn't like her, and it wasn't only fear holding him back.

She'd only been out of his home for seconds and she missed him already, but it didn't seem like there was any hope for them so she was going to have to find a way to get over it, she had a second—or third—chance at life, and she didn't want to waste it because it could be gone in the blink of an eye.

April 11th
10:27 A.M.

He missed her.

Maggie was all he had thought about since he watched her drive away in his best friend's truck.

Theo knew he should have stopped her from leaving. It wasn't that he didn't trust Fletcher to keep her safe, he trusted him with his life and with Maggie's life, but he needed her. In just a few short days, he had become accustomed to her presence, and now that she was gone it was like there was a huge hole in his life.

Watching her walk away was one of the hardest things he had ever done, but he'd done it because she was right when she said he didn't want to hurt her and that if she stayed and he stuck to his decision that they weren't meant to be a couple that she would be hurt.

So he was stuck between a rock and a hard place.

The only way to get Maggie back was to ask her out on a date, open himself up to the idea that maybe third time could be the charm, that things could work out differently, that she was right when she said these feelings she had weren't just because he had saved her life.

But believing that meant opening himself up to being hurt.

Again.

He didn't have a good track record when he slept with friends. Why should he believe this time would be any different?

Maggie was out of his house now and soon she would be out of his life. Things would be awkward and uncomfortable between them and they would drift further and further apart until they were virtual strangers.

That wasn't what he wanted.

He didn't want to lose her.

"Is it okay to come in or are you going to hit me?"

Theo looked up at the sound of the voice and found Fletcher watching him, blue eyes twinkling, smirk on his face, he looked about as worried at the possibility of being hit as he did of the earth suddenly opening up and swallowing him whole.

"Why would I hit you?" Theo asked, feigning an ease he certainly didn't feel. He felt protective and possessive of Maggie, and Fletcher had put himself in the middle of them when he'd allowed Maggie to come and stay with him.

"Oh, maybe because of a pretty brunette with soft skin, huge doe eyes, and long silky waves. Sweet as honey, with a big heart, and an even bigger crush on her own personal hero." Fletcher grinned.

His friend was trying to provoke him, goad him into admitting that he had a crush on Maggie as well, and even though he knew he shouldn't let himself get sucked in, he couldn't seem to think straight when he pictured Fletcher and Maggie alone together in his house. "Did you touch her?" he growled.

"Define touch," Fletcher said cheerfully. "I did help her in and out of my truck, she's such a tiny little thing, and it was hard for her to get up and into it, and I didn't want her breaking a leg trying to get out, not on my watch. And when I got her inside she did throw her arms around me and hug me as she gushed her thanks about me letting her stay at my place until her hotel gets fixed."

Theo growled again as he stood and stalked up and down the room, his hands curled into fists which he resolutely imagined were tied with rope to his sides so he didn't take a swing at his friend. If they hadn't been at the fire station he might have hit Fletcher, just to teach him a lesson that it wasn't nice to try to provoke your friends. But he *was* at the station, and his colleagues *were* just in the other room, so he restrained himself.

"Man, you really got it bad for her." Fletcher laughed like the whole thing was just some big joke to him.

"I don't," he gritted out through clenched teeth.

"Whatever you say, man." Fletcher laughed again. Why was his friend so chirpy this morning? It wasn't like Fletcher wasn't usually in a good mood, but this morning he seemed to be buzzing with energy and he couldn't help but wonder if things had gone further than just a hug between him and Maggie last night.

No.

Maggie wouldn't do that.

She didn't sleep around, not that it was any business of his if she wanted to sleep with Fletcher, she was the one who said she had feelings for him and he was the one who said he only wanted to be friends.

Fletcher might bed anything with breasts, but Maggie was a friend, and he knew what she was going through so there was no way he would put the moves on her, that wasn't the kind of man he was, yet knowing that didn't do anything to dampen the raging jealousy inside him.

"You're jealous," Fletcher said, stating the obvious.

"I'm not," he protested. Jealousy would mean that he felt something for Maggie and he didn't. What he was feeling now wasn't jealously it was ... well, he didn't know what it was.

"She likes you," Fletcher said, growing serious. "Mags has been through enough, it's not fair that you're messing with her like this."

"I'm not messing with her."

"Then why did she call me up and ask if she could come and stay with me?"

"Because she thinks that she likes me."

"She *thinks*?" Fletcher arched a brow. "So you think she doesn't know her own feelings? That sounds pretty condescending if you ask me."

"Well, I didn't ask you," he snapped. "And it's not that I think she doesn't know her own feelings, it's just that she's been through a lot in a short space of time, she's scared, she's hurting, she's emotional, and she's decided that I'm the answer to her problems. If I'm with a woman I want it to be a woman who wants to be with me not a woman who's using me."

"I'm so sick of seeing you mope," Fletcher said. "First it was moping over Talia, then it was moping over Amethyst, and now it's moping over Maggie."

"I don't mope." He pouted.

Fletcher outright laughed at that. "Okay, so you don't have the best track record when it comes to dating friends, but that doesn't mean it won't work out with Maggie. And the difference between Maggie, and Talia, and Amethyst, is that she actually feels something for you that goes beyond friendship, so really you have nothing to lose."

He said it like it was that easy, but it wasn't easy.

Was it?

"Seems to me like you're using the whole friends to lovers thing not working out for you as an excuse."

"I'm not making excuses," Theo said, but even he could hear the sullen tone in his voice.

"You're making this an issue about them. Talia went back to her ex, Amethyst fell in love with someone else, Maggie has just been through a major trauma so she's latched onto you, this is all about them, but it should be all about you. What do you want? Do you have feelings for Maggie? If you do then the past won't matter. What happened with other women won't matter, all that will matter is the way you feel about her. And if you don't feel the same way she does then stop moping about it, you did the right thing to be honest with her and not lead her on. Seems like you have some serious introspective thinking to do, and before you figure things out then maybe you should stay away from Maggie."

With that, Fletcher turned and left, leaving him staring after his friend.

Fletcher was right.

He had been looking at this from every point of view but his own, he'd been so busy making sure he didn't repeat the same mistakes he'd made when he couldn't keep things as casual friends with benefits between either himself and Talia or himself and Amethyst. While he'd been so busy comparing her to the other two women he'd loved he had missed seeing Maggie for herself, for the sweet, kind, beautiful woman that said she had feelings for him.

It had been presumptuous of him to decide for her that her feelings weren't real. Maybe once this was all over and Austin was no longer a threat to her, if she still felt the same way about him then maybe ... maybe he would be willing to risk his heart for another friend.

~

11:04 A.M.

Maggie jiggled her leg up and down as she sat in Abe's office waiting for him. She hadn't slept a wink last night, worrying about nightmares hadn't been an issue, she'd been too wired after confessing her secrets and everything that had happened with Austin, and then everything that had happened with Theo. Fletcher was her friend, and she was just as grateful for him giving her a place to stay as she had been to Theo, but it just wasn't the same.

He wasn't Theo.

She trusted Fletcher to keep her safe, but he didn't make her *feel* safe. Not in the same way Theo did.

Theo was wrong when he said she was just deluding herself that she had feelings for him because he'd saved her life, not once but twice. Theo had made her want to let someone in, he made her want to change her whole perspective on life.

He was important to her.

She had been filled with a need to connect with him that first day after the fire, a need she had never felt for another person. Maybe she had always had feelings for him but she had ignored them until the fire lowered her emotional defenses and she finally let herself feel instead of think.

She knew how she felt and what she felt was real.

Since it wasn't that he was opposed to the idea of sleeping with a friend, or letting things grow from friendship to something more, it had to be her. She was what was different this time around.

What was it about her that he didn't like?

Was it that she had been abused? No, Theo would never let that change his opinion of her. Her lies? No, he had seemed to understand she had been coerced. Did he not find her attractive? No, the heat in his eyes when they'd made love said that he did. The fact that she wasn't as strong and tough as the other women he'd fallen for? After all, his first love had been an aid worker in a dangerous country, and Amethyst Hatcher was a firefighter, all she did was run a hotel.

Maybe she needed to be stronger, tougher, she wanted to respect herself and she hadn't for much of her life. She wanted to like the woman she saw looking back at her when she looked in a mirror. Yes, she'd had awful things done to her, things that would always color her view of the world, but there were lots of things she wanted to improve in herself.

And she would.

But not for Theo.

She would do it because she wanted to have respect for the woman she saw looking back at her in the mirror.

Because she had finally come to realize that she needed to make changes in her life if she wanted to move forward. She couldn't control other people but she could control herself.

Theo had opened her eyes to a lot of things, and even if he wasn't interested in her, he had given her the shove she needed to get her head on straight and realize that if she continued to let fear of Austin rule her life then he would continue to be her abuser.

"Sorry, Mags, I didn't mean to keep you waiting," Abe said as he breezed into the office.

"It's okay," she said, stilling her bouncing knee and straightening in her chair. "Nothing else has happened has it? No more fires?" She hated that Austin was making her live in fear again. Hadn't he done enough to her?

"No, nothing else has happened," Abe assured her as he sat down at his desk. "Did you speak with your sister-in-law?"

"Yes, I called yesterday and again this morning to check in on her and the girls."

"Has she seen or heard from Austin?"

"She says she hasn't since she got the restraining order, that even though he was angry about it he's honored it and stayed away from her." At least Austin was smart enough not to do anything to draw more attention from the cops his way. When he realized that his hold on his wife was severed he had backed off, his thing was going after those weaker than him, and he no longer saw his wife as weak. He was in for a surprise when he finally came face to face with her because she wasn't the same terrified little girl he remembered.

"Did she press charges for what he did to their daughters?"

"No, she used it to threaten him to get the divorce and custody of the girls. She said that if he didn't give her the divorce and if he fought her on custody that she would go to the cops. Austin, he doesn't like small spaces, there's no way that he would risk going to prison even if it meant he had to give up his family."

"Is there any proof that you know of that Austin assaulted his daughters?"

"I think Beth has something on him—insurance of some kind—but she won't tell me what it is, I think she thinks that maybe ..." she trailed off embarrassed to continue. "I think she thinks that maybe Austin might get to me and I'd tell him what it is."

"Well, we both know that won't happen," Abe said confidently. "You would never do anything to hurt your nieces."

His confidence inflated her own, and she nodded. "I warned her that Austin would hurt them, I wish that I'd gone to the cops, told them the truth."

"We all have regrets, Maggie, there are lots of things I'd do differently if I could, but I can't, you've told us everything now and that's going to help us find Austin."

"You really think we can find him before he sets another fire?"

"We're going to do everything we can to make it happen. What about the daughters? Has Austin made contact with them? Maybe tried to approach them when their mom's not around?"

"Beth said she asked them and they both said they hadn't seen their father in weeks. It was four months since Beth found out what he was doing, she filed for divorce immediately. Do you think that Austin has been planning this all this—" Maggie broke off when the door to Abe's office swung open, and Theo walked through it.

"Abe, have you—" Theo also broke-off midsentence when he saw her sitting there. "Oh, uh, Mags, I didn't know you were here."

"We're just discussing her case," Abe informed him.

She just stared at Theo, he looked so good, and she missed him so much it hurt, even though it hadn't even been twenty-four hours since she last saw him. Was he missing her? Did he wish things had gone differently yesterday? Was he even thinking about her at all?

Theo was staring back at her, an unreadable expression on his face. His eyes drew hers in like magnets and she stared deeply into them, trying to discern what was going on inside his head. Ever so slightly his lips parted, and she got the feeling that if they were alone he would have kissed her.

"Did you want something?" Abe asked his brother, breaking the spell, and when she looked back Theo was no longer watching her.

"I was just going to ask how the case was going," Theo replied.

"Maggie can catch you up later."

"Actually, I'm staying with Fletcher," she said.

"With Fletcher?" Abe looked confused. "What happened?"

"Nothing," she said quickly, suddenly awkward now that Theo was here. She didn't want to have to discuss what had happened between them because, to be honest, she wasn't even exactly sure. "I better go. Abe, I'll talk to you later, call me, please, if you hear anything."

"Will do," he agreed, looking from her to Theo and back again as though he was trying to figure out what had happened and what had changed between them.

"The clothes you had in the washing machine when you left, I put them through the dryer, they're on the kitchen table ready for you to get them. I thought since you don't have that many clothes you might need them," Theo told her.

That was so sweet.

He kept sending her mixed signals. He said that he didn't want to be more than friends and yet he did nice things like this for her.

"Thanks, I'll pick them up on my way to Fletcher's." When she said Fletcher's name she noticed him flinch, it looked like he was jealous. Jealous meant he cared, and she fought back a smile.

"Maggie," he started, but she cut him off with a shake of her head as she stood and hurried to the door, she wasn't ready to hear whatever he had to say, he had to sort himself out before he came to her.

"Not now, Theo," she pleaded as she brushed past him, careful not to touch him because even the slightest of touches did crazy things to her heart. She fled the police station as quickly as she could, she had a lot of thinking to do, a lot of soul searching to do, a lot of growing stronger to do, and if Theo couldn't or didn't want to be part of that then for now she had to keep her distance.

~

12:20 P.M.

It felt weird stepping back inside Theo's house.

Especially since he wasn't home right now.

Part of her had been hoping that he would be here, waiting for her, that washing and drying her clothes and leaving them for her to collect was all a ruse just to get her back here so he could tell her that he really did like her.

Maggie sighed and shook her head.

Resolutely, she closed the front door behind her and walked through to the kitchen where she found her laundry sitting in a neat pile. Two pairs of jeans, two sweaters, two pairs of panties, two bras, and two pairs of socks, all clean and dry and waiting for her.

With a smile, she picked up a sweater and lifted it to her face, breathing in the fresh fragrance of the fabric softener. It smelled like Theo's clothes, and she snuggled it close like she was holding onto a piece of him.

She was in deep.

Just as she refolded the sweater in her hands and picked up the rest of the laundry pile, she noticed movement off to her right.

Maggie spun around, but it was already too late, and she found herself looking into the barrel of a gun.

Her brother's piercing brown eyes looked back at her.

"Magsy, long time no see." he grinned at her with that smile she remembered so well from her childhood.

Gun or no gun she had no intention of making this easy for Austin. She wasn't ever going to be that terrified child again, this time she was an adult, an adult who had found the confidence she had been searching for all her life.

"Don't do anything stupid, Maggie," he ordered, as though sensing the change in her. "You have two choices, either you come with me without a fight, or we simply wait here and I shoot Theo Black the second he walks through the door. He won't stand a chance, won't even know I'm here, he'll just walk inside alive and then he'll be dead."

Austin said it so matter-of-factly that she shivered.

He would do it too.

Without a second thought, he would kill Theo just to get him out of the way.

She couldn't let that happen.

So where did that leave her?

She could try to fight him, but that was only likely to get her shot, and then he would wait and kill Theo anyway. Or she could go with him, acquiesce until they got out of here and then when Austin was safely away from Theo she could fight him.

With a meek sigh, she hung her head. "You win."

"I always win, little sister, or have you forgotten that?"

She had never forgotten a single thing that he had done to her, never would, but she knew Austin and she knew how to play his game, how to think he had her under control so he wouldn't see it coming when she made her move.

"So you and Theo a couple?" Austin asked.

"No," she answered honestly.

He looked from the laundry in her arms back to her. "So you let anyone wash your underwear?"

There was no good answer to that so she just shrugged.

"Write him a note, tell him that you want to disappear for a while, that you need some time to yourself to get your head on straight and that you don't want him to try to contact you," he ordered.

Her mind spun as she thought about how she could make the most of this opportunity. A note telling Theo that she had gone off to spend some time alone then might actually convince him that she had. Was there a way to say it so that he'd be suspicious?

Maggie racked her brain trying to think of something, but nothing occurred to her.

"Hurry up, we don't have all day," Austin snapped, coming to stand right behind her and staring over her shoulder.

Since there was nothing she could think of that would communicate that she was in trouble, there was only one other thing she wanted to say to Theo if this was the last time she ever got to communicate with him.

Quickly she scrawled out a note on the notepad he used to write out his grocery list telling him that she didn't regret anything that had happened between them and that she loved him.

"Aww, isn't that sweet," Austin sneered. "My pathetic, weak little sister found someone to love. Only looks like he knows the same thing I do, that you're not worth it."

Maggie had to work to not let Austin's words cut through her. She reminded herself that he'd said them only to try to undermine her confidence.

Well, it wasn't happening.

Toughen up, girl, she told herself. She wasn't weak or pathetic anymore, she had found her power when she opened her mouth and admitted her lies, she was stronger than Austin realized, and while she might not be strong enough to stop him from killing her, she wasn't going down without a fight.

"All right, let's get out of here," Austin snapped when she set the pen down. "You stay close, you don't say anything to anyone, we go straight to the car, you get in the driver's seat, you try to bring anyone else into this and I kill them. You want another death on your conscience?" he mocked.

Maggie nodded her agreement, she *didn't* want another death on her conscience so there was no way she would do anything stupid like call out for help and get some innocent person killed.

With her brother's hand wrapped tightly around her upper arm, and his gun pressed into her lower back, he walked her out of the house and to his car which was parked a little way down the street. She did as Austin told her and got into the driver's seat, he passed her the keys, keeping the gun on her the entire time, and started giving her directions.

As she drove, she pondered the idea of throwing herself from the car, it would be trickier doing it from the driver's seat than the passenger seat. There was a chance that she would wind up more severely injured than Austin when the car inevitably crashed, and he would get her anyway. Her other option was to wait until they got wherever it was he planned on taking her and then make her move. Austin wouldn't be expecting her to do anything and she might be able to use that to her advantage.

When her brother instructed her to turn right at the next street Maggie wondered if he was taking her where she thought he was taking her. He couldn't really be that stupid, could he?

At the next order she realized he was.

He was taking her home.

The house they had grown up in was a small three bedroom ranch on a couple of acres that actually belonged to their grandparents. It was quiet out there, just the way her parents had liked it, just the way her brother had liked it, just the way she had hated it.

If Theo didn't buy that she would disappear, then he knew she was in danger from her brother so surely the first place he would come looking for her would be at the house where her brother's torments had first begun.

Fighting back a smile and playing dumb like she didn't know where they were going because she didn't want to tip him off, Maggie prepared herself for a fight when they got out of the car. She knew a little self-defense. She'd taken some classes a couple of years back because she didn't want to let anyone do to her ever again what her brother had. She knew to aim for the weak spots, groin, eyes, throat, she knew to aim any kicks at her attacker's knees, she knew how to get out of a few holds, and she knew that she had to be smart and use any and every opportunity to her advantage.

"Next right, then drive to the end of the street," Austin ordered.

Maggie did as he told her and then feigned a shocked gasp when she stopped in front of their old house. No one had lived in it since their mother's death when she had gone to their grandparents and Austin had gone to boarding school, and the place was dilapidated and half covered in overgrown vines.

"Home sweet home, hey, little Magsy," he singsonged as she turned the engine off. "This is where it all began, it seems only fitting that this be where it all ends. Don't get out until I come around to your side."

She waited, tense, like a lion ready to pounce on its prey, only her prey was twice her size and armed.

Still, she didn't let the improbability of her beating Austin deter her. If he was going to kill her then he was going to have to work for it. She wasn't going to make it easy for him.

Believing he had her under his thumb he didn't aim the gun at her when he opened her car door for her. She climbed out, took two steps toward the house, then she pivoted and rammed her knee up, connecting squarely with his groin.

Austin howled in pain and surprise, and she turned and ran.

She headed for the surrounding forest because the road would be too quiet. The chances of her finding a passing car were slim, but if she could get out into the forest she might be able to find a place to hide.

Maggie didn't slow when she heard Austin scream her name or when she heard his footsteps echoing hers.

She ignored the stitch in her side and the tightness in her chest and pushed on.

He rammed into her from behind sending them both tumbling to the ground.

"What are you doing?" he screamed. "You think you get to mess with my family and get away with it. You're not walking out of here alive, Maggie. I'm going to punish you until you're begging me to kill you, and even then I won't."

Austin flipped her over onto her back, his hands wrapped around her wrists, pinning her down. Instead of thrashing wildly like every fiber of her being was screaming at her to do, she went still.

Satisfied he had her where he wanted her he loosened his hold, and she struck.

Curling her hand into a fist, she struck out at his throat, her other hand went for his eyes. She missed his eye but her fingernails scraped down his face leaving three trails of blood. Her punch to the throat was partially thwarted as he moved, but she still connected with his chest with a satisfying thunk.

"Maggie," he growled angrily. "What has gotten into you?"

Dragging her to her feet, he wrapped an arm around her chest, pinning her arms to her side, but she didn't need her arms to inflict damage. Austin was a good foot taller than her five foot three frame so she aimed upward and backward and slammed her head into his chin.

Austin cursed and then spun her around, glaring down at her, his eyes were no longer angry, now they were cold. Cold enough to make her shiver like she had just been doused in ice water.

"I'm not playing games with you, Maggie," he said. Then he took hold of her arm, one hand circling her wrist, the other around her elbow, and twisted each hand in the opposite direction, snapping both her ulna and radius in a spiral fracture.

Pain swamped through her, and she retched before unconsciousness grabbed hold of her and yanked her down into its clutches, leaving her completely helpless and at the mercy of her merciless brother.

~

2:52 P.M.

The first thing he felt when he stepped inside his house was Maggie.

Even though she was long gone it was like a part of her lingered, taunting him, teasing him, reminding him that he could have had her if he wanted her and yet he had turned her away, sent her packing, let her believe that there wasn't any hope for them. But he'd been thinking all day about what Fletcher had said, and maybe there was hope after all.

Fletcher had made him realize that he had to look at this as just him and Mags. He couldn't bring Amethyst into it, or Talia into it, because they didn't—nor should they—have anything to do with him and Maggie. He had to figure out his feelings for her because that was really the only consideration right now.

And there *were* feelings involved.

Had she been by to get her clothes?

He assumed she had because she said she was coming by after she left the station. Part of him hoped that she was still here, waiting for him, and if she was he didn't see any other way the day would end other than the two of them upstairs, naked, in his bed.

He'd debated telling her about the clothes and then coming straight here to wait for her. He'd take her in his arms when she walked through the door, hold her close, whisper in her ear that he didn't want her to leave, then scoop her up and take her upstairs to bed.

Whatever else he knew or didn't know about his complicated relationship with Maggie, he knew they had great chemistry and passion in bed.

No, that wasn't true, he knew a lot more than that.

He knew they had a solid friendship, he knew they enjoyed spending time together, he knew she was sweet, and strong, and brave, and that he respected her as well as cared about her.

In the kitchen he found the clothes gone and no sign of Maggie. So she hadn't stayed. Not that he could blame her, but still, he wished that she was here waiting for him.

He'd skipped lunch, and his stomach growled loudly, reminding him quite indignantly of this fact, so he headed for the fridge. He was just getting out some bread and ham to make a sandwich when he saw the piece of paper.

A note.

Maggie was the only one who had been here today besides himself so it had to be from her.

His heart fluttered in his chest as he picked it up, wondering what she had to tell him that she couldn't say to him face to face.

. . .

Dear Theo,

I just wanted you to know that even though you regret what happened between us I don't and never will. I want you to know that I love you. That I'll always love you. I don't know what the future holds, but I do know that no matter what happens you'll always be the man I love. I need some time to myself so I'm going away for a while. I have a lot to process and a lot to work through, and I can't do it here. Please don't try to contact me I need to be alone right now.

Love you
Maggie

Theo stood there, staring at the note in his hands.

It was wrong.

It was all wrong.

Maggie would never go running off now when she knew her brother was after her. If she was going to run she would have done it *before* she told them the truth about who was abusing her as a child, not after. And she would never tell him in a note that she loved him, she hadn't backed down yesterday from having that conversation and telling him she had feelings for him, and she wouldn't back down and tell him she loved him like this. She'd look him right in the eye while she said the words.

Austin must have gotten to her.

That was the only explanation he could think of.

With trembling hands, he pulled his cell phone from his pocket and called Abe. "Get to my house, now," he said without preamble.

"What's going on?" Abe asked.

"Maggie's gone," he said, hating the way the words felt in his mouth. They tasted sour because unlike when she had left his house this kind of gone meant she might never come back.

"I don't understand, I thought she was staying with Fletcher. What do you mean she's gone?"

"She came to get her laundry, she left a note, only I don't think she wrote the note of her own free will. I think Austin has been following her, he used to live here, he knows his way around River's End. He must have seen she was staying here and been lying in wait for her. I think he made her write the note so he could take her and no one would be looking for her."

"I'm on my way, try not to touch anything. If we need to I'll have crime scene come over and search for prints."

"*If* we need to?" he repeated incredulously. "Why wouldn't you get crime scene over here?"

"Because we don't know that we need them yet. Let me take a look at this note."

"What you think I'm holding out false hope that she wouldn't leave?" he demanded. "Do *you* think she'd just up and leave like that?"

"I'll read the note when I get there," Abe said calmly. "Don't do anything stupid like go running off looking for her."

The next five minutes felt like an eternity. Theo read and reread the note a hundred times while he waited for his brother to arrive. When Abe finally came striding through the door, he all but flung the piece of paper at him. "Read it and tell me that sounds like the Maggie you know."

Abe took the note and read it then met his gaze squarely. "What makes you think this isn't something she would write?"

"If she was going to run then why tell us about Austin at all? It would have made more sense for her to go before she told us, because now we know who we're looking for whether she's around or not. She knows that Austin would figure out sooner or later that she's not in River's End and would try to track her down. She'd be alone and vulnerable to him when he came at her next. And ..."

"And what?" Abe prompted when he didn't continue.

"And she would never tell me she loved me in a note," he finished, praying that his brother believed him. If he had to, he would search for her on his own, but he didn't have the resources that Abe as the sheriff did.

Abe studied him with that big brother look he remembered from his childhood, no doubt trying to figure out if he was making an emotional decision or a rational one. Finally his brother nodded. "Okay, I'll call and get crime scene techs over here, we'll dust the place, see if we get any of Austin's prints, I'm sure his ex-wife would be happy to provide us with something of his to get comparison prints from. I'll call Fletcher, see if he's heard from her and ask him to go home and see if she's there. Did she ever get a new cell phone?"

"Yeah, she got one, I tried calling it, but it must be turned off."

"All right, let's go down to the station. We'll work from there," Abe said.

Following his brother outside, Theo was grateful that Abe was holding it together because he felt like he was falling apart. He didn't want these last twenty-four hours to be how things ended between them.

They were halfway to Abe's car when he saw his elderly neighbor in his yard, trimming his rose bushes.

"Mr. Hathoway," he called out, jogging over.

"Afternoon, Theo," the old man replied.

"Have you seen Maggie here today?"

"She was by earlier, around lunchtime, I'd just come out to get back to work. Vivienne is determined to have the best roses in town this year," he said with a big smile. The Hathoways had been married for nearly fifty years, they were both in their seventies but as sprightly as people decades younger.

"Did you see her coming or going?"

"Both."

"Was she alone when she left?" he asked, dreading the answer.

"No, she was with someone, a man," Mr. Hathoway replied.

His stomach dropped, his hands were cold and clammy and he rubbed them on his jeans as though that would help.

Of course it wouldn't.

Maggie was gone.

Her brother had her.

There was no doubt that he was going to punish Maggie for making him lose his wife and kids.

Then when he got bored of that he would kill her.

"Did you get a good look at the man she was with?" Abe was asking Mr. Hathoway. "Could you describe him to a sketch artist?"

"No need to," Mr. Hathoway replied, a glint in his eye saying he knew something big was about to go down. "I know who it was, though I haven't seen him around here in over a decade. She was with her brother, Austin. Didn't seem like she was too happy about the family reunion but she walked down the street aways." He gestured down the block. "And they got into a car and took off together."

Clarity hit him like a brick.

Maggie was no longer just a friend, she had moved out of the friend zone the second she kissed him. Despite his fighting against it, and was now firmly in the relationship zone, which gave her the power to break his heart either by deciding she didn't really love him or by dying. Theo prayed if his heart was going to get broken it would be by the former.

~

4:00 P.M.

It felt surprisingly good to be back here.

Austin had missed this place.

It was both the place where he had been terrorized and victimized and the place where he had been empowered and fought back, turning the tables and becoming the one with all the power.

When their old man had finally gotten busted for beating his wife and daughter—he knew better than to lay a finger on his son by then—and the cops had realized that someone was sexually abusing little Maggie, it had been the perfect opportunity to teach his father a lesson. The man had deserved everything he'd gotten, and he may or may not have sent him a few letters in prison taunting him for what he did to Maggie and pushing him to end his own life. It never hurt to have another thing to hold over someone's head, and guilt over their father's death had helped ensure Maggie's silence. She couldn't tell anyone about her lie without implicating herself.

Behind him, Maggie groaned, and he turned around to face her. "Have a nice nap, little sister?" he mocked.

She was groggy and appeared to be only semi-conscious, she moaned again, and it seemed to take her a long moment to put the pieces together, but he knew the exact second she did because her head snapped up and her gaze met his. "Austin," she croaked.

"Hoping I was just a bad dream?" he asked cheerfully as he strode over to where he had her strung up. "Still have nightmares, Magsy?"

The look on her face said she did, but she didn't cower, she didn't complain even though he knew she had to be in excruciating pain with her freshly broken arm tied above her head, instead she looked him right in the eye. "I don't care what you do to me, Austin, I'm glad I told Beth what a monster you are, and I'm glad she took your daughters away from you, I hope she never lets you see them again."

"Ooh," he said, surprised by the backbone his sister had grown, she wasn't the same petrified kid she'd been when he'd left. "What happened to my quiet little sister that used to cower in the corner?"

"She grew up."

"My, my, did she ever," he gave her naked body an appreciative once over. Maggie had really matured, and while her body was a little thinner than he preferred, he liked his women curvy with nice large breasts, just like his wife, she was certainly a beautiful woman. He lifted a finger, touched it to Maggie's cheek then trailed it down her body, circling her breasts, then gliding across her flat stomach before settling on her hip. "You ever wonder why there are hooks on the ceiling and metal cuffs embedded in the floor?"

"I didn't know they were there, I never came down here as a child," she whispered. She shivered, and he was sure it was a mixture of pain, fear, and revulsion at his touch.

"That's right, daddy hit you, but he never brought you down here because he didn't like little girls, he liked little boys," he sneered.

Maggie's eyes grew wide. "Dad hurt you? You mean like not just hit you?"

"Stupid, naïve, little Maggie. Did you think I was just born a monster?" People—his own parents included—had played with his life, it seemed only fair that he do the same to those smaller and weaker than himself. "I wasn't born a monster, I was molded into one by circumstance."

His hand dropped to his side and he walked around this small room off the back of the basement. It was hidden away where you might not notice it. The door was tucked away behind the washer and dryer, it was a dark, dank little space that used to be illuminated by a single light bulb that hung on a long piece of wire in the middle of the room. It had been broken somewhere along the way so he had set up a lantern in here, the yellow glow cast eerie shadows, making the single metal bed frame with its dirty, stained mattress look even more menacing.

Not that it wasn't already seared into his brain as one of the most menacing places of his life.

"I was six the first time I was brought down here," he spoke aloud but he was really only talking to himself. "Dad was drunk, and Mom was broke, you were just a toddler, screaming away, dad's friends were here, she came up with the bright idea of selling me to them for cash so she could go buy drugs."

"Oh, Austin, I'm so sorry," Maggie whispered.

He didn't want her pity.

He didn't want her sympathy.

He didn't want anything from her but her pain.

Each time he inflicted pain on another it was like a small chip of his own pain disappeared. Who knows, maybe one day he would finally be free of it altogether.

"After that it became a regular thing. They'd bring me down here, tie me up like you are right now." He gestured at his sister whose wrists were tied together with a chain, which was then looped onto a hook that ran on another chain to a hook in the ceiling. Her legs were spread wide, her ankles chained and locked into the hooks on the ground. Her pallor was deathly white, a thin sheen of sweat on her brow, she was trembling, and from the way she kept blinking he knew she was fighting to stay conscious. She was completely bared, completely helpless, completely at his mercy, just like he had been back then.

He remembered that feeling.

Like it was yesterday.

Naked and small, scared and alone in a room with half a dozen drunk men.

"But you know what happens to little boys, they turn into big boys. By the time I was twelve I was the same size as Dad. When he came for me that night I beat him into unconsciousness. He never tried it again."

"When you were twelve I was eight," Maggie said slowly. "And I was eight the first time you came into my room at night."

Austin nodded.

Even before then he used to hurt her, knock her down, push her over, hit her, bite her, hold her head under the water when she took a bath, but it wasn't until he finally realized that he was the one with the power in this house that he really started torturing her.

"It's the food chain, Maggie. Father beats mother, mother arranges for oldest child to be abused, oldest child takes it out on younger child. You just happened to be last, no one to turn to."

"Did Dad ... did he ... did he participate?" Maggie asked.

"Who do you think took the first turn?"

"That's why he believed that he did it to me, because he knew he'd done it to you."

Austin nodded his agreement, it was what he had been counting on. Their father had never denied being the one to sexually abuse Maggie because he knew that he had done it to his son and just assumed he had blacked out while drunk and done it to his daughter as well.

"How can you do this to your little girls when you know what it does to someone?" Maggie looked both disgusted and perplexed. "I get why you did it to me, you were hurting, and I was the only one in the house you could put your hands on. But why your daughters?"

"Because I can," he said simply.

"But—"

"No, no buts," he rebuked firmly, he had tired of this conversation. "You know what they did to me, Maggie?" he asked as he walked around so he was behind her, stroking the length of her spine with his fingertips. "They ripped me apart, tearing my insides to shreds, making me scream until I was hoarse and passed out from the pain. I never did that to you.

Never touched you there, never made you feel that humiliation. Aren't you grateful for that?"

"Y-yes," she stammered, trying to crane her head around to see him, but unable to because it made the chain binding her arms swing and that no doubt sent arrows of pain shooting down her broken arm.

"Has anyone ever touched you there?"

"N-no."

"Today I'm going to take that from you. I'm going to rip you open inside, make you scream, you'll be begging for me to stop and you won't be shown any mercy, just like you didn't show me any mercy when you made sure my wife left me and took away my kids."

Austin was unzipping his pants and positioning himself behind her when he heard the sound of footsteps.

~

4:22 P.M.

They better be right.

They *had* to be right.

If they weren't, it would be Maggie who would pay the price.

"You stay in the car," Abe ordered as he parked in front of the house and got out. His cousins Will and Julian, also deputies, were here too, all of them prepared for what they would find when they walked into the house.

There was no way Theo was sitting out here and waiting.

He was going into that house because Maggie was in there.

His Maggie was in there.

Okay, so it took him until Maggie had been abducted to realize that the reason he was running scared was because he was falling in love with her and if she was wrong about her feelings he would be left out in the cold again.

"I'm coming in," he said firmly, also climbing out of the car. When Abe opened his mouth no doubt to argue, Theo added, "You can lock me in the car, and I'll just break the window. You can handcuff me, but

I'll break my hand if that's what it takes to get free. Maggie is in there, and I'm going in with you. Come on, Abe, I was a Marine, I know how to use a gun and I know what to do in high-pressure situations."

"Fine," Abe huffed. "Will, Julian, you go in the front, Theo and I will take the back door. Clear each room, attic if there is one, Theo and I will check the basement. You stay behind me," his brother ordered when their cousins headed for the front door. "You might know how to use a gun and be used to high-pressure situations, but you're not a cop, and you shouldn't be here."

Since Abe was right and he shouldn't be here he didn't argue on the staying behind him order, anything so long as he was in there when they found Maggie.

He had a concealed carry permit, and he pulled out his gun as he followed Abe to the back of the house and inside. They cleared each room, one by one, it didn't take long because the house was small and mostly empty. Then while Julian and Will headed up to the attic, he and Abe headed downstairs.

The basement was one big room, an old washer and dryer in one corner, stacks of boxes strewn about, but light was spilling out from an open door behind the washing machine, and he could hear voices.

Quietly they crept closer, and when they stepped through the door his heart stopped.

Maggie was by the far wall, her hands were tied and bound with chains above her head, her feet were shackled, she looked woozy and in pain, and one of her arms had obviously been broken because he could see bone.

She was also naked, and her brother stood behind her, his pants unzipped and pulled halfway down his thighs.

Both Maggie and Austin's heads jerked in their direction.

Relief flooded Maggie's face and she sagged.

Austin moved quickly so he was directly behind his sister, which meant that neither he nor Abe could get off a shot without risking Maggie being hit.

"It's over, Austin," Abe said, zeroing in on their perpetrator.

Theo, however, kept his attention focused solely on Maggie. Her brown eyes met his and latched onto them as though he were the only thing keeping her going right now. Her eyes were watery, and pain was etched into every line on her face. He ached to take her in his arms and take that pain away, but he couldn't do anything but stand here and try to offer her silent comfort until they had Austin in handcuffs.

"Get down on your knees, Austin, hands on your head, and you walk out of here alive," Abe said.

"I'm not going to prison," Austin screamed, his voice borderline panicked. "I won't be locked up in another little room."

Sympathy flared in Maggie's eyes, and he wondered if Austin had been held in this very room and abused. If Austin had been abused as a child his sympathy extended only to the child he had been back then, the man who had terrorized Maggie and his own children was a monster.

"You're not walking out of here, Austin. We know what you did to Maggie when you were kids, and we know you're the one who set the fires."

"You don't have any proof," Austin goaded Abe.

"You're here, you took Maggie, hurt her, if nothing else you'll be charged with her abduction and assault. You don't have a choice right now, you will be arrested, and you will be handcuffed, and you will be taken down to the station where you'll be booked." Abe's voice was calm and controlled, he knew they had the upper hand, there were four of them to Austin's one, and as far as he could tell Austin didn't have a weapon on him, because if he did, it would no doubt be aimed at his sister's head.

Austin didn't respond.

They all waited to see what he would do.

Theo kept his gaze focused on Maggie.

She watched him with unbreaking attention.

Abe didn't look away from Austin.

Grabbing Maggie's injured arm, Austin squeezed it, causing her to cry out. "You like the sounds of her screams? If you don't want to listen to her agony you better leave now."

Maggie cried out again when Austin slapped her arm, she squeezed her eyes closed, her breathing a harsh pant as she fought back a sob. "P-please," she begged, but Theo wasn't sure if she was begging them to leave or Austin to stop and turn himself in.

He wouldn't be leaving this room without Maggie in his arms.

Growling low in his throat he launched himself at Austin. The man didn't have a weapon and was preying on their reluctance to do anything that would cause Maggie more pain.

"Theo, don't," Abe screamed, but he ignored his brother.

His single-minded focus was killing Austin.

Killing.

There was no way the man was walking out of here alive.

When he realized that Theo was coming for him, Austin shoved Maggie forward, ripping another agonized scream from her lips as she fell against her chains.

He growled again as he tackled Austin to the ground. The other man fought back but Theo was blinded by a deep, dark, protective rage that fueled him and he slammed Austin's head into the ground over and over again.

He didn't even realize when the man stopped resisting, Maggie's pain made him see red, blurred the world around him into nothing, he needed to make sure her brother could never hurt her again.

Eventually arms wrapped around him and he was pulled backward.

"He's out, Theo, you can stop now."

The words penetrated slowly, working their way through the thick fog of anger until they reached his brain and he looked down at the bloody head of Austin Wilson.

Mollified for the moment that the man was unconscious and no longer presented a threat, Theo shook off Will and Julian's grasps and ran to Maggie, taking her face in his hands and kissing her lightly. "Hey, sweetheart, you're okay now. Help me get her down," he yelled.

Julian appeared at his side, a key ring in his hand. "I'm guessing these will unlock her. You got her?"

Moving behind her, Theo wrapped an arm around her waist and settled her against him. "Yeah, I got her." To Maggie he said, "Just rest, sweetheart, we'll have you down in a moment, lean against me, let me take your weight."

Maggie gave a small nod and leaned into him.

Julian unlocked Maggie's feet first, and as soon as they were free he gathered her into his arms. Her arm was already broken, and when Julian released it and they moved it she was going to be in a world of pain, he wanted her in his arms for that.

A pitiful whimper escaped her lips when the chains were unlocked, and Julian very gently lowered her arms. Tears streamed down her face but she didn't make a sound, just clenched her eyes closed, pressed her lips into a thin line, and shook like she was going to shatter into a million pieces.

"All right, sweetheart, ambulance is on the way. You just hang in there, okay?" He took the blanket Will passed him and carefully wrapped it around Maggie to cover her.

For the first time he spared a glance at Austin and saw that Abe was standing over the man's unconscious form.

The monster wasn't so big and scary now.

It was over.

Maggie was safe.

She was injured, and her arm looked like it would need surgery, but she was going to be okay.

He remembered the words she had written in that note.

I want you to know that I love you. That I'll always love you.

How could she drop a bomb like that in a letter and then walk away with her brother, knowing that he might never see her again?

How would he have felt if she told him she loved him and he never got a chance to say it back because her brother killed her?

"What were you thinking? Telling me you love me and then leaving with your brother?" he demanded harshly, looking down at her paper pale face.

Her eyelashes fluttered as she tried to stay awake. "I'm sorry," she murmured, her voice weak. "I thought Austin was going to kill me and I wanted you to know. I didn't lie about my feelings, and I'm not delusional, I love you, Theo."

He was angry with her for telling him something so big right before she was abducted. He was terrified of her admission because it meant he had to risk his heart for a friend a third time. He was furious with himself for mentioning this now after everything she had just been through.

"Here you take her," he said, dumping—well carefully placing so he jostled her broken arm as little as possible—Maggie in Abe's arms.

He needed space.

He had been friends with Talia, he'd slept with her, and she'd been abducted and tortured before he'd saved her but lost her to someone else.

He had been friends with Amethyst, he'd slept with her, then she'd been taken hostage by a serial killer and fallen in love with someone else.

He had been friends with Maggie, he'd slept with Maggie, Maggie had been kidnapped by her brother.

Why should he believe that this wasn't going to have the same ending?

Why should he believe Maggie wouldn't realize tomorrow or the next day or the day after that she was in love with someone else?

Why should he believe that he wasn't going to get his heart broken and be left out in the cold this time like he had been every other time he'd fallen in love with a woman?

Before he could say or do something that he would regret, Theo left the room, left the house, and started running, trying to outrun his fear, his guilt, and his feelings which terrified him more than anything else.

April 12th
7:17 A.M.

"So this is where you've been hiding."

Theo looked up, not surprised that his brother had figured out where he was but that it had taken him so long to do so.

"You messed up," Abe said, dropping to sit on the ground beside him.

"I know." Theo nodded, hating that he didn't have a good excuse for what he had done to Maggie yesterday.

"You acted like a jerk."

"Thanks, big brother," he growled. "You think I don't know that?"

After leaving Maggie in his brother's arms yesterday afternoon he'd run through the forest for hours, eventually ending up in the place where he and his brothers and father used to go camping when he was a kid. This place held some of the best memories of his life—fishing, cooking over the fire, sleeping in the tent, building forts, climbing trees, telling ghost stories around the fire in the evenings, waking with the sun in the mornings, and playing in the river. He'd loved it out here, and it had been one of the few times his father had really relaxed and just played with them.

They'd come camping here every summer and every term break from school, right up until Abe graduated high school and moved away. He'd been fourteen then and although he would have loved to continue camping it just hadn't been the same without his oldest brother.

This was his happy place, his peaceful place, the place he came when he needed to just be quiet and think.

And right now he had a lot of thinking to do.

"She's doing okay. Had surgery on her arm when they got her to the hospital yesterday, she was out of it most of the night because of the anesthetic, she was already awake when I left and already talking about getting out," Abe told him.

"Sounds like Mags," he said with a tender smile. "And I called the hospital a couple of times to get an update on her."

"You should have been there with her," his brother reprimanded.

"I know. I panicked, okay? I'm not proud of it. You stayed with her?" He didn't like the idea of her having spent the night alone after what she'd just lived through.

"Yes."

"Did she ... did she ask where I was?"

"Yes, several times."

He let out a breath he hadn't known he was holding. "Did she have nightmares?"

"She did, that's why she was awake when I left."

"You left her alone?" he asked sharply, knowing he had no right to judge. He'd left her right when she needed him the most.

"No," Abe replied with a small smile that said he saw the irony in the question. "Fletcher is with her."

That only stoked his jealousy. It was different with Abe, he was happily in love and engaged to be married with a baby on the way, but Fletcher was single and always looking for the next woman to fill his bed.

"What are you doing here, Theo?" Abe finally asked. "It's not like you to run off and leave someone who needs you."

It wasn't.

He had never in his life done anything to let someone down.

Except once.

"Amethyst was sold by her parents where she was raped and tortured and almost died. Talia was on the other side of the world to get as far away from the father who beat her every day. Maggie was abused by both her parents and her brother. It seems I have a thing for women who have been betrayed by their family and abused," he huffed mirthlessly.

"You know why," Abe said quietly.

He did.

There was one other friend he had loved in a very different way.

A friend who had kissed his cheek, giggled, told him she loved him, and then gone skipping away.

He'd never thought about it until last night, but he knew exactly why he seemed to be drawn to women who in his mind needed saving. Women who were strong, tough, competent, able to rebuild their lives after enduring their own versions of Hell. Women who had proven over and over again that he wasn't necessary, that they didn't need him, that he was forever only the friend.

"You have to let it go," Abe continued when he didn't speak. "You have to accept that there was nothing you could have done. Theo, you were four years old. *Four*. What do you think you could have done?"

Nothing.

There was nothing he could have done.

And yet that didn't matter to the guilt.

Guilt didn't thrive on logic it fed off your insecurities, it took your deepest fears and capitalized on them, blew them out of proportion, and repeated them to you over and over again until you couldn't help but give in and surrender to it.

When he was four years old he had been playing at the neighbors' house with the little girl who lived there. She had also been four, a tiny little thing with a mass of blonde curls and the biggest blue eyes a child had ever had. They had been playing hide and seek, and he'd found the perfect spot inside the toy chest in Liliana's bedroom.

It was from there that he had witnessed his friend's rape and murder.

Liliana's father had then shot his wife and then himself.

Little Theo had stayed hidden in the toy box until his mother had come to find out why he hadn't come home for dinner, and stumbled upon the scene.

The murder-suicide he'd witnessed had stayed with him for a very long time. Oh, who was he kidding? It was still with him, he still carried around the guilt on a daily basis.

Yes, logically speaking he knew he had been a four-year-old child, there was nothing he could do against a fully grown man with a gun, and yet Liliana had been his best friend, they'd played together every day, at preschool and then at either of their homes, he'd even married her in a ceremony in the preschool's sandbox. He should have protected her.

The first woman he'd ever let down.

Had Amethyst been a replacement for Liliana? A chance to save the girl this time around?

Had Talia?

Was Maggie?

Maggie was different than Liliana, Amethyst, and Talia. She was quieter, more reserved, she kept to herself, didn't put herself out there to draw in everyone's attention. But she also shared many of the same qualities. She possessed an inner strength that most people could only dream of, she was resilient, she had forged a life for herself against the odds, and not only had she survived but she had thrived.

He respected her, he was attracted to her, and he enjoyed her company. She was his friend but was she also more?

"Maggie dropped the bombshell on me that she loved me in a letter, she never expected to survive her brother. How would I have felt if she died?"

"How would you have felt if she died and you never knew?" Abe countered. "Do you love her?"

He might have fought against it at first, but now the answer was clear as day. "Yes."

"Then you go to her, you tell her that, you apologize, and you explain."

"You make it sound so easy." He turned to study his brother in the early morning light.

"It is. Stop making excuses to push her away, just because Amethyst and Talia didn't return your feelings doesn't mean that Maggie won't. That she doesn't already. Stop dismissing her feelings, stop moping, and stop fighting against it. If you love Maggie, you better get yourself down to the hospital and try to fix things with her before making them worse than they already are. Before you do lose her. I love you, Theo, you're my brother, but Maggie deserves better than you gave her yesterday, than you've given her these last few days."

Abe stood, dusted off the leaves that clung to his jeans, and turned and walked away without another word.

Fear.

The one thing that equalized all people. Old, young, rich, poor, male, female, black, white, fear touched them all.

His biggest fear was failing another woman.

With a heavy heart, he realized he had already failed Maggie, and he didn't know if it was too late to fix things and make them right.

~

8:59 A.M.

Maggie wriggled impatiently on the bed.

She was ready to be out of here.

Well past ready.

Surgery had gone smoothly, a metal pin had been inserted to help hold the bones together while they healed, it certainly wasn't the first broken arm she'd had—all of them courtesy of her brother—so she was practiced at dealing with things one armed, and thankfully this time it wasn't her dominate arm, so as far as she was concerned she was ready to leave. Her arm hurt but it wasn't so bad, certainly not bad enough that it required remaining here in the hospital, and she didn't have any other injuries, which meant it was time to go get out of here.

Where was Fletcher?

He was supposed to be seeing about getting her discharge papers organized so they could go back to his place, but he had been gone almost fifteen minutes now. What was taking him so long? She'd spoken with Levi earlier this morning, and even though he wasn't her doctor here he'd said that since her surgery had gone well and she wasn't going to be going home alone, that if she wanted to leave she could.

That's what he'd said, but maybe he was just trying to trick her, string her along, make her think she was going home only to delay and delay until it was too late and the day was over and she'd be stuck here overnight.

That wasn't happening.

Maggie stood, pleased when she didn't even wobble, and with her arm tucked safely into a sling she stalked over to the door. If Fletcher and Levi were conspiring to keep her in the hospital, she would give the two of them a piece of her mind.

Just as she reached the door it swung opening, bumping into her.

"Oof," she muttered as she stumbled, pain zinged up her arm as she lost her balance and jostled it.

Large hands clamped around her shoulders, carefully away from her injured arm, and steadied her.

Those hands weren't Fletcher's.

They weren't Levi's either.

And they didn't belong to any of the doctors or nurses here.

It was Theo.

They were his hands.

Touching her.

He was here.

All night she had tossed and turned—as best she could anyway with her arm heavily bandaged, an IV, and wires monitoring her post-surgery—waiting, or maybe expecting, him to come breezing through the door at any minute.

Now he was here.

And she was torn between wanting to throw herself into his arms and sob, so relieved that he was back, and telling him to turn around and walk back through the door and out of her life.

For the moment the second option won.

While she didn't tell him to leave she certainly didn't throw herself into his arms, that would be ridiculous, he had dumped her in his brother's arms and disappeared out the door right when she needed him the most. She'd been in blinding pain, her emotions had been in turmoil, and all she had needed was Theo.

But he hadn't been there for her.

"Maggie," he said, slowly and agonizingly like he knew what a mistake he had made and feared it was too late to rectify it.

And it was.

Probably.

Most likely.

No, definitely.

Or not.

Right now she was too drained to figure out if she could forgive Theo or not. So he had left her yesterday, that wasn't the end of the world, he certainly wasn't obligated to be there for her just because she'd told him she loved him. Especially since he clearly didn't feel the same way about her. It was what it was, and she supposed that she could find a way to let it go and maybe one day things could go back to the way they'd been before.

"I'm sorry," he said, his hands still resting on her shoulders. The warmth and weight of them sunk deep down inside her and erased some of the horror of the previous day.

The words *it's fine* were on the tip of her tongue, but she bit them back. She had finally found her strength, she had stood up for herself with Theo, she had stood up to her brother, fought back, and even though she'd had her arm broken for her efforts, Maggie finally felt like she had broken the hold Austin had on her and she had no intention of ever going back to that place.

From now on she was going to make an effort to put her own needs first, treat herself with some respect, and to that end, she stood her ground and stared him down.

A small smile quirked up one side of his mouth in a silent acknowledgment of the changes in her. "You told me you loved me, Maggie, and then you went off with Austin. If that was the last thing you ever said to me I would have felt awful, that's something you say to someone face to face."

"Austin said if I didn't go with him that he would stay in your house until you came in and shoot you as soon as you opened the door," she told him. "You wouldn't have been expecting him, he would have killed you." She didn't care if he was angry with her for it or not there was no way she would have let her brother kill him.

"I wouldn't have been expecting him, I was too busy thinking ..."

That I might be there waiting for him, her heart finished before her head could contribute a thought.

Theo nodded as though he could read her mind. "I was hoping that you might have been there waiting for me."

Her heart soared at his admission. Was there a chance that maybe he did feel something for her after all? "When I got there to pick up the clothes I had hoped you might have been there, that doing my laundry was just a ruse to get me back to your place because you hadn't really wanted me to leave."

"Maggie, I *didn't* want you to leave," he said, his hands on her shoulders kneading gently. "I knew you said you had feelings for me, I just didn't realize that you loved me, I hadn't realized things were that bad."

She stiffened.

Her momentary hopefulness dashed to smithereens, she tried to pull out of Theo's grasp but he tightened his hold.

"That's why I hadn't said it face to face," she said, keeping her tone neutral, hiding the heartbreak she felt. "You think me loving you is a bad thing.'

"That didn't come out the way I meant. Maggie." He sighed as though he didn't want to tell her this, then gently slid his hand down her good arm until he reached her hand. Curling his fingers around hers, he led her over to the bed and sat her down, sitting beside her and keeping his grip on her hand. "There's something you need to know about me."

Panic and concern momentarily wiped away the hurt. "Are you okay?"

"I'm fine, it's not like that, only my parents and brothers know about this, it's the reason my family moved here when my dad retired from the Navy. We used to live next door to a family with a little girl my age, her name was Liliana and we were the best of friends. One day I was playing at her house, hide and seek, I was hiding she was seeking only her father interrupted. I learned this later, but he had recently lost his job after he became addicted to painkillers following a car accident. He'd fallen asleep at the wheel, his older daughter was in the car, she'd been killed. He shot Liliana, then his wife, then himself, I watched the whole thing from the toy box."

"Oh, Theo," she whispered, squeezing his hand. What an awful thing to have witnessed, especially for such a small boy. Theo had only been four when he and his family had moved to River's End so this had happened before that.

"I loved her, in a four-year-old kind of way. She was my best friend, I still remember her cries as her dad held a gun on her, asking him what he was doing, begging him not to hurt her. I wanted to help her, but I couldn't move. I was frozen in place. I remember the thump as her little body hit the floor and her sightless eyes staring back at me. I wet myself, I remember shivering as it made me cold. After I left yesterday I went out to a spot where my dad and brothers and I used to go camping. While I sat out under the stars I realized that it seems I have a thing for women who my mind sees as needing saving. I guess in my mind it's trying to save them because I couldn't save Liliana."

"I see," she said slowly, not at all sure that she did. Was he trying to tell her that he didn't feel anything for her because she was just another victim representing the little girl he had lost? "Are you trying to let me down gently?"

"What? No. The opposite."

"The opposite?"

"I think I'm in love with you."

"No," she contradicted immediately. As much as she wanted to hear him say those words she didn't believe them. At worst, he felt sorry for her, and at best he was on the rebound, and there was no way she wanted to be in a relationship with someone who was only with her so he wasn't alone. "You're in love with Amethyst. I'm not going to be your second choice just because you can't have the woman you want."

"I thought I was in love with her, but now ..."

"Now what?"

"I'm not so sure. Maybe Amethyst was right, maybe all we ever were was friends with benefits. What Amethyst and I had was sex, but what you and I had, that was making love."

"Sounds like semantics," she said skeptically. She wasn't in the mood to play around, they'd danced around their feelings enough the last few days and she wasn't doing it anymore. She had been upfront and honest with him and she wanted the same courtesy.

"I know that you have every reason to doubt me, I know I messed up, Mags, I know I hurt you, I know I pushed you away. It was because I was scared. Maybe at the back of my mind I knew that nothing was ever going to happen with me and Talia or me and Amethyst and that made it safe. But you're different. Whatever you need me to do to make it up to you I'll do, whatever you need me to do to earn your trust and your heart, I'll do."

That was sweet, and she couldn't deny that he was saying all the right things and that her heart was cracking accordingly, but ...

She still wasn't sure he was being honest.

What made him so sure that he'd been wrong about being in love before but was right about it this time?

"You're not convinced," he said, a statement not a question but she nodded anyway. "I'm asking for a second chance, Maggie, a chance to see if we really are falling in love with one another. I want you to move back in with me while you heal and while your hotel gets rebuilt, we can spend time together, go on a few dates, take things as slowly as you want. You've been honest with me, and I'm trying to do the same. I'm trying to be honest with myself as well. Remember when you asked me if I would take back sex with Amethyst if I could, and I told you that I would if it meant that we'd be able to remain friends and things wouldn't be awkward between us."

"Yes, I remember." She also remembered him telling her that the two of them having sex had been a mistake.

"Well, I wouldn't take back sex with you even if it meant I had to lose you because those moments when our bodies were joined were the best moments of my life. I don't just want to be your friend, Maggie, I want to be with you, I want us to be a couple. It's up to you, what do you want? Do you want to see this through, give us a chance? Or did I mess things up beyond repair?"

Her heart already knew the answer.

Austin and her parents had made her afraid of men, of relationships, and she'd acted accordingly, locking off that part of herself and her life.

Theo made her want it all.

He was nothing like her parents or her brother, he'd hurt her by holding back, but she understood that he had his own demons to battle. And he'd hurt her yesterday when he left her when she'd needed him, but was it worth ruining what could be the best thing to ever happen to her by holding onto that pain?

Stubborn pride or happiness.

When she put it like that there was only one answer she could possibly give.

~

9:13 A.M.

Why was she taking so long to answer?

That had to be a bad thing.

Theo tried not to fidget as he waited to see if Maggie was willing to give them a chance. He knew he had no right to ask, he'd given up that right when he'd abandoned her yesterday, but he was praying that she was forgiving enough to give him a chance to make it up to her. He was prepared to work for it, he didn't expect that she should make it easy on him, but he would prove that he was committed to her if she let him.

She hadn't pulled her hand away, and he had to take that as a good sign but the seconds ticked by, fifty-four of them to be precise—which might not seem like much, but when your entire future was hanging in the balance it felt like an eternity—before she drew in a breath.

"Okay," Maggie said.

"Okay?" he repeated because she wasn't smiling and didn't look happy which made him both confused and uncomfortable.

"Okay, we can give us a chance."

"You don't have to sound so excited about the possibility."

Maggie huffed a chuckle, and then a smile finally lit her face. "I didn't mean it to come out that way. I *am* excited about the possibility, I guess it's just that after the week I've had it sounds too good to be true, and I keep waiting for the other shoe to drop."

"I hate that I'm to blame for some of that." He'd made so many mistakes these last few days. Maybe he'd made so many mistakes his whole life. So many years trying to save people because he hadn't saved Liliana, so many times he had thought he was in love only to now realize he had been wrong. Talia and Amethyst had been friends who he had subconsciously believed could help him find absolution for his part in Liliana's death.

But Maggie was different.

Maggie had slipped through his defenses and managed to snag a hold on his heart.

"What are you thinking?" Maggie asked, her eyes studying him as though he was a puzzle that she was trying to figure out.

"That I let stupid fears get in the way of what was growing between us. I was afraid that you would decide that you were wrong and all we were was friends, and I'd be out in the cold again."

"Why is that stupid?" she asked, cocking her head.

Theo shrugged. "It just is."

"So, what? The big, bad, former Marine turned firefighter who saves people every day is embarrassed about being insecure?"

This was heading into distinctly girly territory.

Okay, that was probably a little sexist, but he'd been raised in a military family, he'd been a Marine, he was a firefighter, he didn't really do well with the whole vulnerability and discuss your feelings thing.

However, he sensed that Maggie needed to see his vulnerabilities, and for her he'd do it even if he wanted to shove the whole thing deep down inside and forget about it. Probably not the wisest move, that's what he'd been doing these last twenty-five years, and it hadn't helped. Maybe he should try a different approach.

"You suffered a trauma," Maggie continued. "A major trauma, and in your most formative years, it was bound to help shape the kind of person you grew up to be. And for the record, I very much like the person you are. I also suffered a major trauma while I was growing up and it affected me too. Why is it you can accept that what my parents and brother did to me scarred me in ways that will never heal, but you can't accept that you have scars that will never heal? What, is it only women who are allowed to be affected by things like that?"

"No, of course not. Anyone can be affected by trauma." How many big, strong, tough men he had served with had been fighting demons that wanted to eat them alive? Theo knew that trauma hit anyone, no matter who they were, with enough force to crush them.

"You were passed over several times, you're hesitant at being hurt again, it's perfectly normal. I get it. I thought that my lies that led to my father's death meant I shouldn't be allowed to find happiness, and I was going to stick with that until a certain arrogant firefighter burrowed beneath my defenses."

"Arrogant, huh? I seem to remember you saying you kinda liked the person I was," he teased.

"Actually, I think I said I very much liked you," Maggie corrected with a grin. "I just want to let go of the bad parts of this week and hold onto the good parts, like kissing you."

"Sounds like an invitation." He winked.

"You are correct."

Mindful of her broken arm, he circled an arm around her waist and tugged her sideways so she was sitting in his lap, then his mouth dipped and his lips claimed hers. He'd intended to keep the kiss light in deference to her injury, but Maggie pressed her body close, and hooked her good arm around his neck, kissing him like she intended things to go a whole lot further.

"Mags," he warned against her lips, "as much as I'd love to get you naked right now someone could come into your room at any moment."

"Oh," her face fell, "I forgot we were here."

Theo laughed, it felt so nice to be with someone who actually wanted him back. For now, he was done analyzing the impact of what he had witnessed as a child had had on him, and the relationships that never were with Talia and Amethyst, he had a gorgeous, smart, sweet, sexy woman and he wanted to enjoy every second of her.

"Fletcher was supposed to be finding out about my discharge papers, if I can get out of here we can go back to ..." she trailed off as uncertainty filled her eyes. "Are you sure you want me to come home with you?"

"The thought of you going to Fletcher's leaves me insanely jealous even though I know nothing is going on between you two. I want you with me."

Maggie relaxed. "I was hoping you would say that, but I didn't want to pressure you."

"You're not pressuring me, I never should have let you go, Mags," he admitted.

"It's okay." She cupped his cheek in her hand and rested her forehead on his. "You had been burned before, and you were wary of believing me when I said I was falling for you, but you believe me now, don't you?"

"You betcha, babe," he promised, tilting his face so he could kiss her again.

Groaning in frustration, Maggie said, "Are Fletcher and your brother waiting outside my room for some sort of signal from you that they can come in? Because I really want out of here."

He could see it written into every fiber of her being just how badly she wanted out of here, and she wasn't wrong, he had asked Levi and Fletcher to give him some time alone with Maggie so they could talk things through, but it hadn't even been twenty-four hours since she was kidnapped and assaulted, she needed to stay here a little longer.

"I have a deal for you," he said.

"Yeah?" She raised a suspicious brow.

"You need to stay here a little longer, rest a bit, make sure your arm is doing okay, how about you sleep for a while and then tonight I'll bust you out of here and take you back to my place. Deal?"

She considered for a moment. "Will you lie on the bed with me while I sleep?"

"Sweetheart, there's nothing I'd rather do than hold you in my arms."

"Okay." She sighed long-sufferingly, but he knew that if she was even contemplating it then she had to be feeling worse than she was letting on. "Deal."

"That's my girl." He kissed her again, liking the idea of Maggie being his girl, not in the sense that she was property and he owned her, but that they were together and she wanted to be with him. "I'll help you lie down." As carefully as he could, he helped her stretch out on the bed, but he noticed her wince. "You want me to get Levi, ask him to give you something for the pain?"

"Nope," she replied, snuggling into the mattress. "I have all I need. You."

Stooping, he touched his lips to Maggie's forehead. "I love you, Maggie."

She smiled tiredly up at him. "Love you too."

Moving around to her other side so he was on the same side as her good arm, Theo laid down beside her. Maggie immediately snuggled against him, her head on his chest, and gave a contented sigh.

"Sleep now, baby, I got you, nightmares can't get you while I'm here." With an arm tucked around her to keep her close, Theo stroked her hair softly, and in less than five minutes her body had gone limp against him as she drifted off to sleep. Closing his eyes, he left the feel of Maggie in his arms, her breath warm against his neck, her hair tickling his nose, and quickly joined her in slumberland.

~

6:38 P.M.

Someone shook her.

Snapping her out of sleep.

"Maggie, it's okay, it's me, Theo, you were thrashing around, having a nightmare, but you're okay, you're in the hospital."

As sleep cleared from her eyes, she saw Theo's concerned face looking down at her. It was sweet that he worried about her, but there really hadn't been any need to. A slow smile crossed her face as she thought about what had filled her dreams.

"What are you smiling about?" Theo asked, clearly confused. "Mags? You with me?"

"Oh, I'm with you," she giggled, looping her good arm around his neck and dragging him closer so she could kiss him.

He groaned and took her mouth again, kissing her slowly as though he wanted to savor every second of it. "I thought you were having bad dreams again, and ..."

"And?" she prompted when he didn't finish his sentence. Theo was stretched out beside her on the bed, propped up on his elbow, one hand was curled around the back of her neck and the other rested lightly on her stomach. She could stay like this forever. But there was a glint of concern in Theo's eyes and that put her on edge. "What's wrong?"

"Nothing on my end."

"You think I think something is wrong?"

"Do you?" Piercing hazel eyes studied her, probing for an answer but she had no idea what he was talking about.

"What do you mean?"

"You were having bad dreams," he replied as though that explained everything.

She hadn't been, but she wanted to know where this was going. "And?"

"Well, the other night we spent together, you said that was the only night you hadn't had nightmares, and this is the second night we spent together and you had bad dreams again, I wasn't sure if that changed things, you know ..."

"I literally have no idea what you are talking about."

"Whether it changes things between us."

"You mean like I won't want to be with you now because I had nightmares while sleeping in your arms?" She almost told him that was ridiculous but she could see he genuinely thought it was a possibility. Although she wouldn't wish insecurity on anyone, seeing Theo struggle with it—and trust her enough to let her see it—bolstered her own confidence. Theo had family support, had dedicated his life to saving people, always had women throwing themselves at his feet and yet he still doubted himself. If he did then maybe it didn't make her so weak that she did too. "I wasn't having bad dreams, Theo."

"You weren't? You were thrashing about though."

"Not in fear, I wasn't having nightmares. I was dreaming about you—me and you together, in bed, doing wicked things to one another. And even if I was having bad dreams that wouldn't change anything between us. Okay, so that night I slept in your arms and didn't have nightmares was the first time I realized that maybe I felt something more for you than friendship, but it's not what I'm basing my feelings on now. You make me feel special, you make me feel important, you make me feel beautiful, you walked through two burning buildings to save me. I know it's your job, but you didn't even have any of your gear the second time. I want out of here, now, when we get back to your place I'll show you what I was doing to you in my dream," she said, gently pushing on his shoulders.

"You sure you're ready to leave?" Theo asked, brushing his fingers tenderly around the wrist of her good hand where there were reddish-purple bruises from the chains.

Maggie quickly pushed away those thoughts before they could come barreling down upon her and crush her.

She wasn't ready to think too deeply about Austin and everything he had told her and everything he had done to her, she knew she would have to address it at some point but she wasn't ready. For now, she just wanted to be glad she was alive and that she wasn't alone anymore. She had Theo and he knew about every dark facet of her life and seemed to want her anyway.

"I feel good, I don't need to be here, I have my follow up appointments booked with my surgeon and I'm ready to get out of here. I just want to move on with my life, now that I finally have one."

"All right, I'll go tell Levi you're ready to get out of here. Be right back." He kissed her and helped her sit upright, then kissed her again before he disappeared out the door.

She missed him.

It was silly, he'd been in the room just seconds ago, and yet as soon as he left her sight she realized that she missed him.

Maggie smiled, it was nice to have someone to miss, she'd been alone for so long, she'd always felt alone, in her parents' house, and even with her grandparents, because she had secrets and sometimes keeping secrets was lonely. But now she had Theo, he'd always been a part of her life, he'd been a good friend, and now she knew he was going to be an amazing boyfriend and maybe one day a husband.

"All right, Mags, you're officially busted out." Theo grinned when he breezed back into the room. "Let's go home."

She froze halfway standing up.

Home.

All week she'd been grieving the loss of her home, her hotel and her apartment were gone, and as much as the loss still hurt she realized that Theo's house had become home to her.

"You okay?" Theo appeared at her side, his arm slipping around her waist as he drew her close.

"Yeah, I'm good, great actually, let's go home."

Taking her hand and entwining their fingers, she and Theo left the hospital and found his car in the parking lot. They sat in companionable silence as Theo drove them to his house while she daydreamed about what they would do when they got there. This time would be so much better than when he'd driven here there after the first fire because this time it wasn't just something to make her forget what had happened, this time it was making love to the man she was falling in love with.

"Come here." Theo had parked his truck in his driveway and come around to open her door for her. He gathered her into his arms before she could protest—not that she would protest—and was carrying her down the path to the front door. "Fletcher dropped your clothes off here, so if you want you can take a bath, or if you need to sleep I can tuck you into bed, or if you're hungry I'll make you something to eat."

"Oh, I'm hungry but not for food," she said, nibbling on his earlobe.

"Maggie," Theo groaned as he carried her through the door and closed it behind them. "You just had surgery on your arm twenty-four hours ago, there is no way we are having sex tonight."

"But I want you." She pouted.

"You're going to be the death of me, Maggie Wilson," Theo said with a dramatic sigh. "Maybe I can give you a little something."

"Oh yeah?" she asked, arching a hopeful brow.

"You better be a good girl and not get yourself overexcited, the last thing we need is to have to take you back to the hospital because you hurt your broken arm with sex," Theo ordered with a wink as he laid her down on the couch.

"And if I'm not?" She giggled.

"Then I'd have to punish you," he teased.

"I like the sound of that," she said as a delightful shiver tingled through her from head to toe.

"You might be regretting those words in a minute, sweetheart," Theo warned as he took hold of her sweatpants and eased them down her legs. Her panties were next and without her even realizing it her hips lifted off the soft sofa cushions, wordlessly begging for attention.

Theo pressed a hand to her stomach holding her in place. "Patience, patience," he murmured as his head dipped between her legs and before she could tell him to hurry up his mouth was on her.

His tongue was like a magic wand, working her into a frenzy in minutes, and just as bright lights began to fill her vision he stopped.

"Theo," she groaned, trying to twist her hips to find where he'd gone, but he held her firmly in place.

"I thought you wanted me to punish you," he said with a bemused smile. "Not enjoying your punishment?"

"You better finish what you started, mister. Please," she begged because she was at the point where she was ready to do or say anything as long as his mouth was back on her.

"I'm a sucker for your begging, Mags," he told her and then finally his mouth was on her again. Working its magic, making that out of this world feeling build in her stomach, stars began to twinkle above her, and then in a rush, pleasure exploded inside her, rippling through every inch of her body.

By the time she floated back to earth Theo had slipped the sweatpants back on her and snagged a blanket, snuggling her on his lap and tucking it around them both. Maggie tried to move but he tightened his hold on her. "I want to touch you now," she said.

"Not tonight, Mags, you gave me everything I wanted, watching your face as you came. Now you should get some rest."

"I slept away most of the day already," she protested, but a badly time yawned nearly cut her face in two.

"You've barely slept in a week, or I guess really you've barely slept in a lifetime. Just rest now, Mags, let me hold you in my arms, be your knight in shining armor and slay your dragons because you've been doing that on your own for long enough. You're not on your own anymore, sweetheart, you're not fighting those dragons alone, you have me, and I'm not going anywhere. Ever."

Those were the nicest words anyone had ever said to her.

She'd never had anyone who wanted to stand by her side and help her fight her past before.

"I love you, Theo," she said as she kissed his jaw and then tucked her face against his neck.

"Love you back, Mags."

Although she could have sworn she couldn't have slept again so soon her eyes were suddenly very heavy, and they fluttered closed. Theo's hand was rubbing circles on her back, and his breath was warm against her forehead. For the first time in her life she didn't dread sleep's hold on her and let herself drift away content in the knowledge that Theo's arms were her safe haven.

Return to River's End as Levi Black does what he swore he'd never do and falls in love again in the fifth story in this gripping, emotionally charged romantic suspense series!

Also by Jane Blythe

Detective Parker Bell Series

A SECRET TO THE GRAVE

WINTER WONDERLAND

DEAD OR ALIVE

LITTLE GIRL LOST

FORGOTTEN

Count to Ten Series

ONE

TWO

THREE

FOUR

FIVE

SIX

BURNING SECRETS

SEVEN

EIGHT

NINE

TEN

Broken Gems Series

CRACKED SAPPHIRE

CRUSHED RUBY

FRACTURED DIAMOND

SHATTERED AMETHYST

SPLINTERED EMERALD

SALVAGING MARIGOLD

River's End Rescues Series

COCKY SAVIOR

SOME REGRETS ARE FOREVER

SOME FEARS CAN CONTROL YOU

SOME LIES WILL HAUNT YOU

SOME QUESTIONS HAVE NO ANSWERS

SOME TRUTH CAN BE DISTORTED

SOME TRUST CAN BE REBUILT

SOME MISTAKES ARE UNFORGIVABLE

Candella Sisters' Heroes Series

LITTLE DOLLS

LITTLE HEARTS

LITTLE BALLERINA

Storybook Murders Series

NURSERY RHYME KILLER

FAIRYTALE KILLER

FABLE KILLER

Saving SEALs Series

SAVING RYDER

SAVING ERIC

SAVING OWEN

SAVING LOGAN

SAVING GRAYSON

SAVING CHARLIE

Prey Security Series

PROTECTING EAGLE

PROTECTING RAVEN

PROTECTING FALCON

PROTECTING SPARROW

PROTECTING HAWK

PROTECTING DOVE

Prey Security: Alpha Team Series

DEADLY RISK

LETHAL RISK

EXTREME RISK

FATAL RISK

COVERT RISK

SAVAGE RISK

Prey Security: Artemis Team Series

IVORY'S FIGHT

PEARL'S FIGHT

LACEY'S FIGHT

OPAL'S FIGHT

Prey Security: Bravo Team Series

VICIOUS SCARS

RUTHLESS SCARS

Christmas Romantic Suspense Series

CHRISTMAS HOSTAGE

CHRISTMAS CAPTIVE

CHRISTMAS VICTIM

YULETIDE PROTECTOR

YULETIDE GUARD

YULETIDE HERO

HOLIDAY GRIEF

Conquering Fear Series (Co-written with Amanda Siegrist)

DROWNING IN YOU

OUT OF THE DARKNESS

CLOSING IN

About the Author

USA Today bestselling author Jane Blythe writes action-packed romantic suspense and military romance featuring protective heroes and heroines who are survivors. One of Jane's most popular series includes Prey Security, part of Susan Stoker's OPERATION ALPHA world! Writing in that world alongside authors such as Janie Crouch and Riley Edwards has been a blast, and she looks forward to bringing more books to this genre, both within and outside of Stoker's world. When Jane isn't binge-reading she's counting down to Christmas and adding to her 200+ teddy bear collection!

To connect and keep up to date please visit any of the following

Printed in Great Britain
by Amazon